Perfect EMBRACE

MASON CREEK

NEW YORK TIMES BESTSELLING AUTHOR

KAYLEE RYAN

The following story contains sexual situations and strong language.
It is intended for adult readers.

Cover Design: Opium House Cover Designs
Cover Photography: Lindee Robinson
Editing: Hot Tree Editing
Proofreading: Deaton Author Services
Paperback Formatting: Integrity Formatting

Prologue

LAKEN

Sixteen years old

"**G**AH! DID YOU SEE GRAYSON?" I ask my best friend, Justine. "Holly is so freaking lucky." We're standing in the bathroom of our high school, Mason Creek High. As sophomores, we don't usually see the juniors and seniors too much. However, there are times, like today, that we get a glimpse and, well, let's just say, seeing him walking out of the office and watching his tight end, which has nothing to do with his position on the football field, just made my day.

"That she is," Justine agrees, running her Chapstick over her lips.

Before I can gush about how gorgeous he is, one of the bathroom stalls opens, and out walks Holly. As in Grayson Davis's girlfriend, Holly. I cringe, ready for her to give me hell for checking out her boyfriend. Holly and Grayson are both seniors. My sister, Leni, is a junior, and I don't hate it when I get to tag along with her to ogle the hotness that is Grayson Davis. However, I would never speak those words to anyone but my best friend, Justine, or my sister.

"H-Holly—" I start, and she smiles. Not a sneer, but a genuine smile.

"I happen to agree with you." She winks.

"I'm so sorry. I would never— I mean, I was just looking—and I'll shut up now."

Justine squeezes my shoulder, letting me know she's there with me through this embarrassing ordeal.

"There is nothing wrong with looking, Laken." She steps up to the sink and washes her hands.

I didn't even know she knew my name. "I'm sorry," I say again.

She turns to look at me, and I think this is it. The tongue lashing I was expecting. Not that that's her thing. I don't know much about Holly, other than she's dating the hottest freaking guy in our school. "Don't apologize for looking. It's not illegal. You weren't plotting this evil plan to seduce him," she jokes. "It's all good. I promise. And honestly, if I were you, I'd be looking too." She shrugs.

"Still, I shouldn't have said that. Not here." I bow my head.

"Hey." She steps toward me. I can hear her drying her hands and the hard-crinkly brown paper towels the school places in the bathrooms. "You did nothing wrong. I know what Gray and I have is good. Even if you were plotting the demise of our relationship, it wouldn't work." She shrugs again and tosses the paper towel into the trash can. "Have a good day, ladies."

As soon as the door closes, Justine looks at me with wide eyes. "Did that just happen?"

I hold my arm out to her. "Pinch me."

She does, and I indeed feel the sting. "She's so freaking cool."

"She really is. Couple goals right there."

"Truth. No wonder he's head over heels in love with her." That's the other thing. Grayson isn't afraid to show the entire school that Holly is his number one. He walks her to class, sits with her at lunch, kisses her at halftime before heading to the locker rooms. The list goes on and on.

Grayson Davis has set the bar high and has helped me realize that's what I want. I won't settle for a guy who doesn't love me like he loves Holly.

Chapter 1

LAKEN

"THANK YOU," I SAY TO the UPS driver as my cell phone rings. Rushing around the counter, I grab my phone and smile when I see my sister, Leni, and my adorable nephew, Trace's, smiling faces. I hit Accept and place the phone to my ear. "You two ready to move home yet?" I ask.

"Aunt Laken!" Trace exclaims, making me laugh.

"Hey, bud."

"Guess what?"

"What?" I ask with all the enthusiasm my five-year-old nephew expects.

"Mommy and me are going to get ice cream."

"You are? What flavor are you going to get?"

"Aunt Laken..." He laughs. "You know that chocolate is the bestest."

"I knew you were my favorite nephew."

"Yep!" he agrees. I don't remind him that he's my only nephew. That's just details. "Mommy wants to talk to you," he says, and then he's gone.

"Hey." Leni laughs.

"He's a ball of energy today. Are you sure ice cream is a good idea?"

"It's still early," she says. "Besides, he's been doing really well with keeping his room clean and getting his toys picked up. This is his reward. And, well, I just wanted some ice cream." She chuckles.

"So, you two ready to move home yet?"

"He starts school in the fall."

"That's all the more reason to come home. Mason Creek is where you need to be with your family. I miss you, and I miss getting to see my nephew grow up. You know Mason Creek is a great place to raise a family."

"I know, but it somehow feels like I failed."

"What? No way, Leni. It means you miss your family, and you want to move home. You love this town. I know you do. Mom and Dad miss you too. Think about it. I love it when you come to visit, and that it's been more frequent. I'd love it even more if you lived here full time. We could have girls' night every week."

"I have been thinking about it."

"Good. That's all that I can ask for." The chime on the door alerts me to a customer. "I have to go. I'll call you later. Kiss Trace for me, and tell him to enjoy his ice cream."

"Will do. Talk to you later."

"Bye," I say, ending the call and turning to face the counter.

"Miss Waken!" two gorgeous little girls greet me.

"Hello to you too," I reply with a smile. "How are you today, ladies?" I ask them, making eye contact with their grandmother Christine.

"We're so good," Harlow replies. She's just a little shorter than her twin sister, Hayden. It took me a few visits to be able to tell them apart, and now it's easy to see. Harlow is also the more outgoing twin. Both girls have energetic personalities, but Hayden seems to be okay with letting her sister take charge. Hayden is also just a little taller than her sister.

"Nana Chrissy said we can both get a new book!" Hayden exclaims.

I can't help but smile at the two of them. "Well, you better start looking." The words are barely out of my mouth before they're sprinting off to the children's books. "How are you, Christine?" I ask their grandmother. It's usually Grayson's mom, Jackie, who brings them into the store.

"Those two"—she shakes her head—"are impossible to say no to. Grayson tells me that I spoil them, but I just—" She shrugs as tears well in her eyes.

Reaching out, I grab her hand, giving it a soft squeeze. "I'm so sorry for your loss." I don't know what else to say. It's been three years since Grayson Davis lost his wife and the mother of his twin girls. Holly was also Christine's daughter. Her pain radiates from her. Then again, she lost two daughters that night. Holly's sister, Heidi, was in the same accident. Mason Creek is a small town. We all see how she clings to the twins, and not one single person can blame her for that. It's her only connection to her daughter Holly.

"How about a coffee?" I ask.

"That would be wonderful." She smiles. "I was headed to Stitches next door, and those two insisted on stopping. I know Jackie usually brings them. They talk about you and this place all the time."

"About once a week," I tell her as I get to work making her coffee. I have a variety of coffee and tea, as well as a few bottled drinks and pastries for my customers. No, I don't make them. I mean, I know how to bake, but not on this level. I stop by the bakery across town every morning and grab a small selection to serve to my customers throughout the day. At the end of the day, I usually walk what's left of the treats, if there are any, to the firehouse. Those guys work hard and enjoy the treats. At least they seem to.

I mean, giving them some leftover pastries is the least that I can do after the show they give me. I live in a small apartment above the bookstore. The firehouse is just down the street. The guys wash the trucks behind the building closest to my building, and I'm not ashamed to admit that I've peered out my window a time or two, taking in the show. Trust me. You would too if you were me.

"Here you go." I hand Christine her usual.

"Thank you, Laken."

"Nana, look!" Hayden comes running. "It's bunnies." She smiles.

"I see that. What about your sister? Did she find one?"

"Yep!" Harlow skips over to where we stand and holds up her book.

"Sheep. Good choice, ladies."

"Will you read to us?" they ask at the same time.

"Girls, Nana has to run next door to the seamstress to see if the shirt I dropped off for Pap is ready. Maybe another time."

"You can leave them here," I tell her.

"I don't know. I can't imagine Grayson liking that."

I try not to let her comment sting. I know he's protective of his daughters. "The offer stands."

"Just... let me call him." She steps away, and I hear her talking on the phone. She comes back and smiles. "He's just getting off work. He's going to be right over. As soon as he gets here, I'll walk next door."

I try not to let it get to me that the sexy Grayson doesn't want me left alone with his children, but it kind of stings. Then again, I understand. He lost their mother tragically, and those two angels are all that he has left of her. The sting, though, it's still there.

"Why don't you ladies go grab a spot in the reading nook and I'll be right there?"

"He's protective," Christine says once the girls are out of earshot.

"It's fine." Walking behind the counter, I reach for the sign that says *Reading in session, please ring the bell for service* and place it on the counter. "All set." Grabbing my coffee, I smile at her. "He's their father, and even though we've all lived in this town our entire lives, I'm a stranger to him and to them."

"You're hardly a stranger."

"Maybe." I shrug. "Grayson and I went to school together, but our circles don't really follow one another. Besides, they're his daughters. He has every right to say who can and cannot spend time with them."

She nods. "Thank you for understanding." As soon as the words are out of her mouth, the chime over the door sounds and in walks the man himself.

"Hey, Chris." He gives her a tired smile and kisses her cheek. "Where are the girls?" He looks at me, albeit briefly, before his eyes scan the room. Giggles filter from the back of the room, and he smiles.

"They love it when Laken reads to them."

Something flashes in his eyes, and although brief, I can see the sadness and the pain. "They talk about it a lot," he tells her before turning to me. "Laken."

I'm well aware that I'm a twenty-eight-year-old woman. However, the teenager in me who had the biggest crush on one Grayson Davis is swooning over how he says my name. I've never heard my name fall from his lips, and let me tell you, it's sexy as hell.

"Grayson." I nod and turn my attention back to Christine. "It was good to see you," I tell her.

"You know they won't let me live it down if we miss a day. That was the first thing they asked when Grayson dropped them off this morning. They were sure to remind me that Nana Jackie brings them here every Thursday," she explains. "I'm going to go say goodbye."

Together, the three of us walk to the back of the store where the reading nook is located. The girls look up and spot their father and come running. I watch as he drops to his knees and catches one in each arm, hugging them close.

"Daddy, we missed you."

"Are you here to read with Miss Waken? Wait, we don't have to leave, do we?" This is from Harlow.

"No, Daddy. We have to read. It's Thursday. That's our story day," Harlow explains. "Nana Chrissy bringded us here. Just like Nana Jackie."

"It's Thursday," Hayden echoes.

"We're not leaving. Nana had some things to do, and I just happened to be getting off work."

"Yay!" they cheer and step out of his hold.

They each grab one of my hands and pull me toward the reading nook. It's more of a cozy area than a nook, but nook sounds so much better. It's a small corner in the back of the store. There is a round, bright green, super soft, plush rug for us to sit on.

"Girls, I'm leaving," Christine calls after them.

"Bye, Nana!" They wave at her.

"All right, are we ready?" I ask them.

"Yes! Mine first," Hayden says, thrusting her book about the scared little bunny toward me.

"Once upon a time—" I start but stop when Harlow yells for her dad.

"Daddy, you have to sit on the circle during story time," she tells him with all the attitude of an adorable little four-year-old. She even gives a little huff at the end of her demand as if she's irritated he didn't already know.

"Yeah, Daddy, come sit." Hayden pats the soft green carpet next to her.

"You're more than welcome to join us," I tell Grayson. "Or, if you'd prefer, there's an adult lounge." I point to the two small leather loveseats that are in the opposite corner of the store.

"Daddy." Harlow stands and takes him by the hand, pulling him to the carpet. "Sit with us."

He smiles down at her and does as he's told. She climbs into his lap, and he snuggles her close. When Hayden moves beside me, I expect her to go to him as well. However, I'm surprised when she lifts my arm and settles on my lap.

"You can read now, Miss Waken," she says, tilting her head back to look at me.

I can feel his eyes on me, but I don't dare look. Instead, I smile down at his daughter and begin to read. It takes a lot of effort, but I pretend like it's just the girls and me as I read to them, changing my voice to emulate the characters. They giggle here and there, but for the most part, they're quiet little angels while I read.

"My turn!" Harlow climbs off her dad's lap and moves toward me with her book in hand.

Without saying a word to one another, Hayden stands from her place on my lap and takes her sister's place on their dad's, while Harlow settles on mine and hands me the book.

"You ready to read about sheep?" I ask.

"I'm ready." Harlow tilts her head back against my chest, and I can't help it. I give her a little squeeze before I begin to read. When we're finished, the girls stand with their books, and I expect happy smiles and a flurry of activity, but what I get is sad faces.

I'm still sitting on the floor, as is Grayson, but both girls are now standing with their books in their hands. "Hey," I keep my voice soothing, "what's with the sad faces?"

"Nana left," Hayden whispers.

"And she didn't give you the card. That's what Nana Jackie does so we can take them home."

It dawns on me that they're sad they don't get to keep the books. "Well, guess what?"

Their curious little minds can't help but ask "What?" at the same time.

"Today, those"—I point to the book in each of their hands—"are gifts."

"I can pay for them," Grayson says.

I turn to look at him for the first time, and I can't read his expression. His green eyes are watching me intently. "I insist," I tell him. I force my eyes back to his daughters. They don't need to see me drooling over their dad. "These books are my gift to you." The words are barely out of my mouth before two little bodies, adorned with smiles that could give the sun a run for its money, lighting up the sky, are wrapping their little arms around me.

"Thank you, thank you, thank you," they say in unison, and I have to admit this twin thing is a little freaky.

"You're welcome. Now, there is one thing you have to do for me," I tell them.

"What?" Harlow asks.

"You have to read every day. It's good for your mind." I tap my temple. "And your soul." I place my hand over my heart.

"Miss Waken." Hayden giggles. "We can't read. We're this many." She holds up four fingers.

"Hmm." I pretend to think of a new plan when this was my plan all along. "Well, I guess you're just going to have to look at the pictures and make up your own stories." There is nothing like the imagination of a child, and I know these two little angels putting their minds together could come up with some interesting stories. "How about next week, when Nana Jackie brings you in, you read to me? You can tell me the stories you create?"

"Yes!" they say together, bouncing on the balls of their feet.

Glancing over at Grayson, he has his head slightly tilted, watching the three of us intently. If I'm not mistaken, there is a hint of a smile at the corner of his mouth. He's even sexier now than he was when I had my crush on him in high school. He's tall, toned, and tatted, and I realize I'm staring at him. Averting my gaze back to the girls, I block out the way the ink swirls around his arm and his muscles bulge in his T-shirt.

"Girls, we should let Miss Laken get back to work."

"Okay," they begrudgingly agree.

After a round of hugs, the girls each take a hand and pull me from the floor—after a few tries, of course, since we have to make a game out of it. Once I'm standing on my own two feet, their little arms wrap around my legs. "Bye, Miss Waken. Thank you for the books."

"I'll see you next week, ladies, and you're welcome," I say, patting their backs.

"Ready?" Grayson asks. He's now standing next to us.

The girls release me, and each takes one of his hands, their books in the other. "Thank you." He nods at me.

"You're welcome," I say as they turn and walk away. I follow along slowly behind them. Not so close that I feel like a stalker, but close enough that I can watch him in those worn fitted jeans as he walks away.

When the door closes, I push thoughts of the sexy Grayson Davis and his adorable twin daughters out of my mind and get to work putting away my delivery. I don't know what it is about him that makes me feel like my sixteen-year-old self again. I had the biggest crush on him in high school, but that was years ago, and we're both adults now. He's a single father. He shouldn't be making me feel all warm and gooey inside from just being in his presence.

I think Justine is right. I do need to get out more. I make a mental note to call her. It's definitely time for a girls' night.

Chapter 2

GRAYSON

I'M STARING AT THE ALARM clock, watching as time slowly ticks by, and willing my mind to turn off so I can go to sleep. It was a hard shift today at work—an accident about a mile out of town that ended in air-carrying the driver.

I got word about an hour ago that the kid, just seventeen years old, is going to be okay. He's one of the lucky ones. I love my job. I love helping people. That's what drove me to become a firefighter. A year ago, I was promoted to captain, which is almost unheard of at my age. Thoughts of what drove me to work harder filters through my mind, and I shut it down. I don't need to go *there*. Not tonight.

A loud crack of thunder booms, making it feel as though the house is shaking, and I know what will happen next. I can't hear the pad of their little feet over the storm as they race down the hall, but I know they're coming. Sure enough, not a minute later, my bedroom door is being pushed open, and the bed dips as the twins crawl in beside me.

"Daddy?" Harlow asks.

"Yeah, sweetie?" I raise my head to look at her.

"Can we sleep with you?" Hayden asks from behind me.

"On one condition."

"What?" they ask together. It used to freak me out, the way they talk at the same time, saying the same things and finishing each other's sentences. Hell, sometimes they don't even say a word. There's some kind of freaky twin vibe that they just know and understand what's coming next. At first, it freaked me the hell out, but now I'm used to it, it's cool as hell. I especially like to watch others' reactions to them. It's very entertaining.

"I need snuggles." I finally give them their condition.

A round of giggles and "Done" comes from both of them. Rolling to my back, I spread out my arms, pulling each of them into my embrace. Their little heads rest against my bare chest.

Another smack of thunder, and they both jump and snuggle in closer. "Daddy's got you," I croon to them.

My daughters are my world. I never imagined I'd be doing this dad gig on my own, and it's tough most days. I have a lot of support from my parents and my late wife's parents as well. I remember in those first days after losing their mother, my mom told me something that has stuck with me. It takes a village to raise a child. At the time, I thought she was crazy, but I don't know how I would have done it without all their help.

"Sissy?" Harlow speaks up.

"Yeah?" Hayden asks.

"Let's make up a story like Miss Waken said."

"Once upon a time," Hayden starts.

"—there was a bunny and a sheep that was bestest friends," Harlow adds.

The girls continue on with their story as my mind wanders to Laken. I've seen her around town. I went to high school with her and her sister, Leni. I know who she is, but I don't know her. However, she seems to be well acquainted with my daughters. I was shocked when Hayden crawled into her lap. I was ready to give her the lecture about stranger danger, one we've had many times, but she was so relaxed with her. And the way that Laken smiled at her, it was like a knife to my chest.

They're missing out on the love of a mother. They're missing her presence in their life, and that guts me. They're very attached to both sets of grandparents, but Laken is the first adult other than family, and my best friend, Ryder, I've seen them act that way with. Then again, other than Ryder, they haven't been around any other adults. At least none that they spend a lot of time with. However, it appears that their weekly visits to the bookstore with Nana Jackie have turned into something more between the three of them. So much so, there were able to convince Christine to take them this week. Mom usually has them on Thursdays, but she picked up a shift at the dentists' office to cover for one of the other receptionists.

"The end." Hayden giggles.

"Did you like it, Daddy?" Harlow asks.

"The best story I've ever heard."

"We hafta tell Miss Waken. Daddy, can we do One More Chapter?" Hayden asks.

"It's getting late. How about you do another chapter tomorrow?" Children's books, at least those for their age, don't even have chapters. I don't know where they come up with this stuff.

"No, silly." Harlow giggles.

"Miss Waken's store. That's the name, right, Daddy?"

Schooled by my four-year-old daughters. "That's right," I tell them. How could I forget the name of the damn store? "How about we get some sleep, and we'll see what tomorrow holds?"

"Okay," they respond together. "Love you, Daddy."

"I love you both to the moon and back." I place a kiss on the top of one, then the other's head, and snuggle them closer.

I push the sadness out of my mind even though it lives in my heart for my daughters and their mother they'll never remember. I push the pain to the bottom of my chest that Holly is gone and missing our daughters and the incredible little humans they are. I see so much of her in them, sometimes so much it makes it hard to breathe. I miss her every single day.

Giggles. That's my alarm clock this Saturday morning. I pretend to still be asleep as the girls giggle from their spots on either side of me.

"Daddy sleeps loud," Harlow says, making her sister laugh.

"Pap does too!" Hayden says, and another fit of giggles ensues.

Lifting my arms, I tickle their sides as they squirm. "What are you two monsters doing talking about me while I sleep?"

"You sleep loud!" They laugh hysterically as I move to my knees and tickle them both. Their backs are on the bed, and their little bodies squirm from my tickle monster hands.

"You unleashed the tickle monster." I make my voice deeper. Bending down, I blow a raspberry on Hayden's belly where her shirt has ridden up and then the same to Harlow on hers.

"Mercy!" Harlow yells.

"I have to pee!" Hayden squeals.

That's all it takes for me to stop. I'm not about to wash the sheets when I just did it earlier this week. "Go potty," I tell them, giving them a break from the tickle monster.

"I'm going to Daddy's bathroom!" Hayden slides off the bed and makes a mad dash for my room.

"Hurry, sissy, I gots to go too," Harlow informs her sister.

"Go use yours," I tell her.

"I wanna use yours," she says, dancing around.

Finally, Hayden appears, and Harlow rushes past her like a hurricane. Hayden climbs on the bed, and I snuggle her close. I will never tire of snuggles from my girls. I'm already dreading the day they're too cool to hug dear old dad. I know it's coming, and I am in no way ready for it.

"Daddy, my belly's angry," Hayden tells me.

"Hmm, maybe we should feed it?" I suggest.

"Mine too!" Harlow runs and jumps on the bed, joining us.

"All right, so what are we eating today?" I ask them.

"Jitters!" they both cheer, and I can't help but laugh.

"Jitters it is. Go brush your teeth, and I'll grab you some clothes."

"No, we want to pick," they say.

"Okay. You can pick." It's hard to tell what they're going to be wearing today. However, over the last four years, I've learned to pick and choose my battles. "Go get ready. Daddy's going to grab a shower. Do not go downstairs without me." I point at them, reminding them of the rules. I have to keep them close.

"We know," they say dramatically.

I have a vision of them as teenagers rolling their eyes at me and amping up their already teenager-like attitudes. "Keep it up, and we'll be eating here."

"Nope!" they say and scramble off the bed and race down the hall to their room.

I rush through my shower, not wanting to leave the girls to their own devices for long. Pulling on some shorts and a Mason Creek Fire Department T-shirt, I go in search of the twins. I hear giggles coming from their room and stop just inside the doorway. There are clothes thrown all over the room in between their two twin beds. The house has three bedrooms, but they insist on sharing a room. So the third bedroom is their playroom.

"What's going on in here?" I place my hands on my hips and try to be stern and not let my smile pull at my lips.

"Daddy, we don't have nuffing to wear," Harlow says theatrically.

Lord help me. "Well, I guess that means no Jitters. You can't go in your pjs."

"No!" they whine.

"Choose, girls, and when we get home, you're cleaning your room. What have I told you about throwing your clean clothes all around your room?"

"Sorry, Daddy." Harlow is the first to apologize, followed quickly by her sister.

"Get dressed. I'm going to grab what we need for your hair." I walk out of the room and head for their bathroom, grabbing what I need to tame their dark curls. I'm still in a constant state of learning, and I can braid but not French braid. The girls keep asking me to learn, and I've watched a few YouTube videos, but every time I try, it turns out looking... well, not like it does at the end of the video.

When I make it back to their room, they're both dressed in blue jean shorts and tank tops. The clothes actually match, which is a blessing. They've been known to want to wear their princess play dresses, and I'm the pushover who lets them. Mom tells me that I spoil them, but I'm a man. What do I know about four-year-old girls and what's right in fashion for them?

Thirty minutes and a half a bottle of detangler later, their dark curls are pulled into pretty decent-looking ponytails, if I do say so myself, and we're loading up in the truck heading to Java Jitters for what's sure to be a sugary breakfast. It's not something I do all the time, knowing it's not the most nutritional, but Java Jitters has, well, the best java, and I could use a cup or four today.

The drive to Java Jitters is short. Just enough time for the girls to sing along to one song on the radio. After parking my truck on the street, I turn to face them. "You can get out of your seats, but don't open the doors. I'll come around to get you." About a year ago, they decided they were big girls and were going to open their own door. They chose the door closest to the street. Luckily I was just at the back of the truck and made it to them in time, but it gave me nightmares for weeks that something was going to happen to them. Not the first time in the last three years that I've praised the fact that Mason Creek is a small town and not a busy city. My girls climbing out of the truck onto a busy street could have turned out much worse. I'm aware I'm overprotective, but I will make no apologies for it.

I've already lost their momma. I can't lose them too.

"Ready?" I ask, pulling open the door. I lift Hayden out first, and just like I've taught her, she wraps her arms around my leg while I lift Harlow out.

"Hold hands, sissy," Hayden says, and they link hands while Hayden reaches up for mine. That's how the three of us walk into Java while I hold the door open with my free hand.

"Miss Waken!" they exclaim, dropping my hand and running across the small dining area to get to Laken.

"Girls!" I call out, but it's no use. Laken has already pushed out her chair and is embracing them both. All three of them are wearing huge smiles.

"Hey, ladies," she greets them. "Are you here for breakfast?"

"Yep," they reply proudly.

"Girls, you can't run away from me like that," I scold.

"But, Daddy," Harlow protests.

"It's Miss Waken," Hayden adds.

"I understand that, but you know the rules."

"Sorry," they mumble.

I nod and then make eye contact with Laken. Her hazel eyes are bright as she glances up at me. "Hey, Grayson."

She's beautiful.

It's not the first time I've had that thought, but it ends there. She's easy on the eyes, but I don't have time for more. My daughters are all that I have time for after a full week at the station.

"The three of you should join us."

I turn to look at who offered the invite to see Justine Samson.

"We don't want to impose," I say, placing my hand on each of my daughters' shoulders, ready to guide them to the counter to order.

"Please, Daddy," my twin angels plead.

"That's crazy." Justine smiles. "Do they do that a lot?"

"They do," Laken answers before I get the chance. "It's really something... the way they are connected."

"Miss Waken, we wroted a story," Harlow tells her.

"You wrote a story?" Laken corrects while managing to ask with interest while pretending to be surprised, even though she told them to do so. "Hayden, did you help?"

"Yes. We tolded it to Daddy last night when the sky was angwy," Hayden tells her.

Laken smiles at them, and then me and my breath hitches in my lungs. "You told your daddy," she corrects her gently. "I'm sure it was the best story ever," she says enthusiastically.

"It was," they tell Laken.

"Come on, girls, let's get some breakfast."

"And you need coffee, right, Daddy?" Harlow asks.

"That's right, baby. Daddy needs coffee." I laugh.

"We'll be right back, Miss Waken, and... what's your name again?" Hayden asks Justine.

"I'm Justine. Miss Laken is my best friend."

"My sissy is my best friend, oh and my daddy," Hayden tells her.

"And Miss Waken too," Harlow announces.

Justine and Laken chuckle softly. "Come on, monkeys, let's get some breakfast." I guide the girls to the counter and order breakfast and a large black coffee. By the time we're through the line, Laken and Justine are standing to leave.

"You're leaving?" Harlow asks, sounding on the verge of tears.

"I'm sorry. Justine and I are going shopping in Billings today. I'll see you Thursday when you visit me at the store. I want to hear that story."

"Daddy, can we go shopping in Biwings?" Harlow asks.

"Not today, sweetheart." I let her down gently.

Laken bends her knees to talk to them at eye level. "You two need to keep your daddy company. I think he's been missing you while he's at work all week," Laken tells them. She glances up at me. "I think he needs lots of hugs and maybe even for you to clean your rooms."

The girls gasp in surprise. "How did you know about our messy room?" Hayden asks her.

"I was a little girl once too. Do you think you can do that for me? Then on Thursday, I want to hear your story," she reminds them again.

"Okay." My girls agree all too easily and wrap their arms around her neck. "Bye, Miss Waken," they say, stepping back.

I watch as she stands to her full height, adjusting her purse on her shoulder. "It was good to see you, Grayson."

"Laken." I nod. I can't manage more than that as I process how easily she handled my daughters and how good she is with them. "Be safe," I manage to add.

"Always." She nods, then turns her attention back to the girls. "See you soon, ladies." With a final wave from both her and Justine, they walk out the door.

By the time we get home, I have a text message from Ryder.

Ryder: *You might want to take a look at this.*

Attached is a link for the *MC Scoop*. I fight the urge to roll my eyes, but I click the link anyway, knowing without even looking it's going to be about me.

Love Jitters

One of Mason Creek's most eligible bachelors, a single daddy of two adorable little girls, just might be off the market. Rumor has it he and our town's beloved bookstore owner have been getting well acquainted. From storytime to breakfast at Java. There looks to be quite the connection between our bookstore owner and his daughters.

Stay tuned!

Damnit, Tate. That girl is always sticking her nose where it doesn't belong. I really don't need the entire damn town gossiping about me. About me and Laken. It's bad enough that I don't understand this pull I have toward her. Having them throwing in their two cents isn't going to help.

Chapter 3

LAKEN

"What was that?" Justine asks as we exit Java Jitters.

"What was what?"

"That. Grayson's daughters adore you."

"They're little girls who are excited to have the attention of an adult for a few hours. Grayson's mom, Jackie, brings them by every Thursday afternoon. I read to them while she takes a break and reads on her own."

"Do you read to everyone's kids? Or is it just those two?" She raises her eyebrows, and I laugh.

"All the kids, if time allows. Thursdays are always a slow day for the shop, and I don't know. It just kind of started, and now it's our routine. Jackie wanted to get the girls into reading."

"What's this story they're talking about?" she asks.

I go on to explain their visit to my bookstore, One More Chapter, on Thursday afternoon. I even tell her how the four of us sat in the reading nook and read two stories.

"That explains it," Justine says, pulling out of the parking lot.

"Explains what? Why are you talking in riddles?" I ask, amused.

"The tension between the two of you."

"Tension? What tension? Are you feeling okay?" I ask my best friend. I'm hoping like hell she believes my lack of understanding. I'm not ready to talk about what she describes as tension between Grayson and me. Surely, it's just all in my head.

"Go on. Pretend like it's not there. I know what I saw."

"How long has it been since you've had an eye exam?"

"Laugh it up," she tells me. "There is something there."

"You're projecting my crush. I've always had a thing for him. However, we're adults now. He's got two little girls who are his world to focus on."

"Single parents can date," she counters.

"I know they can, but Grayson, he's still grieving. He's not the same lively person he was before losing Holly. There is no timeline on mourning the love of your life."

"I agree with you, and I'm not saying that he's not still tore up about losing her. My heart breaks for him and those little girls. However, I know she would want him to move on. If it was me, I would want that for him and for those girls."

"He'll move on when he's ready."

"And what are you going to do when he moves on with you?"

"Have you been drinking?" I ask, partly just to mess with her and the other part to change the course of the conversation. Grayson has always been my crush, so to speak. I knew in high school that he and Holly were it for one another, and she was so nice it was impossible to hate her. I would never have done anything to jeopardize what they had, and still today, no matter how sexy he is with his toned body and a full sleeve of tattoos, I still won't. Without question, his daughters are his number one.

"Stop." Justine grins. "I'm just saying. I could feel the energy."

"What you were feeling was the energy from those two little girls of his. I'm telling you, they are so sweet, and I'm sure such a handful. I'm kind of excited to hear the story they came up with. I have no doubt that their imaginations ran wild."

Those little angels already own a piece of you.

"There is no energy. I'm just being a friendly neighbor."

"You're not his neighbor."

"You know what I mean. That's what we do in Mason Creek. We look out for the town and the people in it. If me reading to his daughters once a week brings them joy, then that's what I'll do."

"Come on now, don't pretend that it's just those girls who love it."

"You're right. I love it. I love books. It doesn't matter if it's a children's book, a romance, or a mystery and anything in between. Hence the reason I opened my own bookstore."

"I just want to go on record that I called it."

"You're crazy."

"You should go for it. Make it happen."

"He's not ready."

"Is he not ready? Or are you afraid you might fall?"

"What's with all this deep conversation?" I'm not afraid of falling in love. In fact, I want that. However, I've crushed on Grayson Davis since I was a teenager. I've watched him struggle losing his wife and now become a single father. It's not as simple as us dating. There are two other little hearts involved.

Justine shrugs as she pulls into the parking lot of the mall. "I guess I just want you to be as happy as

Tucker and me. I know you think that the odds are stacked against you. I know he lost the love of his life, but he's young, and he can find love again. Give me one good reason why he can't find that love with you?"

I don't reply because I don't have an answer. In high school, he was my crush. Now that I'm an adult, there is still some attraction there. I mean, he's a firefighter, his body is muscular and carved to perfection, and the ink... the ink is sexy as hell. I don't know if it's Grayson that I'm crushing on or the idea of Grayson. He checks off all of my boxes. Not to mention, he's an amazing father to those two little girls. I don't know any woman who would see him with his daughters and not swoon over him.

Just as we're getting ready to exit the car, I get an alert on my phone from the *MC Scoop*. I usually ignore it—in fact, I should delete the app—but something tells me to open it. I regret it as soon as I do. Tate is at it again; only this time it's me, and Grayson, and his daughters she's speculating about. "Ugh," I say, handing Justine my phone. She reads the small blurb, and throws her head back, laughing. "It's not funny."

"It kind of is," she replies.

"Yeah, well, Tate is a pain in the ass with this blog of hers."

"Come on." She reaches for her handle. "It's out there. There is nothing you can do about it now. Once people see the two of you aren't together, the speculation will die down."

I hope she's right, I think to myself as I shove my phone back into my purse and climb out of the car.

"You should wear that denim skirt tonight," Justine says, pulling in front of the bookstore.

"You think so?" I ask with amusement. "And what are you wearing?"

"Hopefully nothing once Tucker gets home." She wags her eyebrows.

"I mean to Pony Up." I can't help but shake my head at her antics. It's so good to have her back home. I missed her so much while she was living in New York.

"I'll wear mine too." She points to the back seat of her car. "They're cute."

"Agreed. Okay, what time are we meeting?"

"I'll just swing by and pick you up. Tucker is going in early to set up. I'll be here at seven*ish*."

"Perfect. Thanks for today. It was fun."

"See you in a couple of hours." She waves as I shut the door and step back. With my arms full of bags, I struggle with unlocking the door to the store. I usually only use the back entrance after hours, but it was just easier for her to pull out front and drop me off. Besides, this is closer, and these bags are heavy.

Finally, I manage to get the door open. I drop my bags inside and pull the door closed, locking it. Loading my arms up again, I drag my purchases upstairs to my apartment. It's a small studio-style space. I have my queen-size bed in the far back corner and the kitchen in the opposite corner. The rest is living space, a couch, bookshelves, a small television, and my reading chair. It's one of those huge round ones that swivel back and forth. It's big enough for another person and me. Depending on who the person is, we'd still have room. I love it. I keep my "one more chapter" pillow and a super soft throw that Leni got me for Christmas a few years ago draped over the back. It's the perfect reading spot.

When I bought this place, this space was the deciding factor. I always had dreams of owning a bookstore, and when Nana passed, she left my sister, Lenora, and me a small inheritance. I wanted to purchase a home of my own and a business. This building allowed me the freedom to do both.

It takes me some time to unpack all of my purchases from today. It's been forever since I've gone shopping like this. I'm just about to strip down for a shower when my cell rings. I smile when I see it's my sister. "Hey, you."

"What are you getting into tonight?" Lenora asks me.

"Heading to Pony Up with Justine. You?"

"You want some company?"

"What?"

She laughs. "I asked if you wanted some company."

"Are you here?" I ask, my voice rising an octave.

"I'm here."

"What? Why didn't you tell me?"

"I wanted it to be a surprise."

"What about Trace?"

"He's here too. And all of our stuff."

"Explain," I demand of my sister.

"You were right. This is where I want him to grow up. This is where I want to be. So, I tied up some loose ends, called Mom and Dad, and here we are."

"You're home?" I ask, tears welling in my eyes. "You're really here?"

"I'm here."

"I'm mad at you for not telling me, but I'm thrilled that you're back. That you're home for good."

"Good. You need to help me find a place of my own. I love Mom and Dad, but I don't know if I can handle living with them again after being on my own for so long."

"Done."

"So, Pony Up?"

"Yes. Justine is picking me up at seven, but I'll call her and tell her that we'll meet her there. I'll pick you up. This is your night to cut loose. And it's long overdue, Leni. Mom and Dad have Trace covered. You get to cut loose, and I'm here for it," I say, making her laugh. "Go get ready. I'll be there around seven."

"Fine." She pretends to be irritated. "You twisted my arm."

"You're damn right I did. See you soon." I toss my phone on my bed and do a little dance around the bed. I can't believe they're home. Finally. I've missed my sister and my nephew. He better get ready for Aunt Laken to spoil him rotten. I mean, I do from afar, but having him close is so much better.

Pulling up to Mom and Dad's, I climb out of the car and rush up the steps. Well, not really rush, this denim skirt and these ankle boots don't really leave room for rushing, but I do hustle as much as my outfit will allow. I don't bother knocking as I push open the door.

"Where is my favorite nephew?" I call out. I hear Trace's sweet laughter and follow the sound.

"I'm in here!" he replies, laughing.

I make my way to the living room, following the sound of his laughter, and he rushes me, wrapping his little arms around my waist. "You have to stop growing," I tell him, returning his embrace.

"I missed you, Aunt Laken, and guess what?"

"What?" I ask, running my hands through his hair.

"We live here now."

"What?" I feign shock.

His little head bobs up and down so hard I'm fearful he may have whiplash. "We do." He turns to look over his shoulder at my sister. "Right, Mommy?"

"That's right, sweetie," Lenora replies, tears shimmering in her eyes.

"Well, I think this calls for a sleepover at Aunt Laken's house."

He gasps. "Can we do that?" he asks.

"Of course we can. Not tonight. I'm taking Mommy to dinner, but soon."

"Yes!" He jumps up, throwing his hands in the air as he cheers.

My throat swells with emotion. I knew I missed them, but I didn't know it was this bad. I step away from Trace, and my sister sees me coming. She stands, and we hug each other tightly. "I've missed you," I whisper.

"I've missed you too."

"And me." Trace squeezes his little body between us, making us laugh.

"Definitely you," I assure him, stepping back.

"Trace, you be good for Mamaw and Papaw," Lenora says in her best mom voice.

"I will."

"You ready?" I ask her.

"So ready." She smiles.

After another round of hugs, we're out the door and on our way to Pony Up. I'm barely out of the driveway when she mentions the *MC Scoop*.

"Please tell me Mom and Dad didn't see it."

"Of course they did. How do you think I knew about it? I'm the new girl in town, remember," she replies.

"Shit," I mutter under my breath.

"Relax. Mom was excited, and Dad just said that Grayson is a good man."

"We're not together!" I protest.

"I told them that. Apparently, Tate has a knack for fishing out information and reporting it, and usually, she's spot on when it comes to relationships."

"Seriously?" I ask her. "Let me guess, Mom told you that?"

"Yep. I guess she nailed it when it came to Wyatt and Sadie, and even Justine and Tucker. According to Mom, the list is a mile long of her love connections."

"What? That's absurd. She doesn't make love connections."

"She might not make them, but it sounds like she might be good at sniffing them out."

"Well, she's sniffing up the wrong tree this time."

"It's barking up the wrong tree, and I don't know… sounds like she has a talent for this kind of thing."

"Can we forget about Tate and the *MC Scoop?*"

"If you say so." She grins, then smashes her lips together, pretending to zip them up and throw away the key.

"No way!" Justine shouts as we walk through the door of Pony Up. "Leni!" She pushes back on her chair and comes rushing toward us. "It's so good to see you," she says, wrapping my sister in a hug.

"Good to see you too, Just," Lenora replies.

"Come sit. And you—" Justine points at me. "How dare you keep this from me." There's no heat behind her words.

"I just found out myself. She called and asked if we wanted company." I shrug. "I didn't think you'd mind."

"Hell no, I don't mind. Come on, you two." She links her arms through both of ours and leads us to the table where our friends Olivia and Charlotte are already sitting.

"Hey." Lenora waves.

"Good to see you," Charlotte and Olivia say at the same time and dissolve into a fit of laughter. It appears they did a little pregaming with the alcohol before we got here.

"Get me some of what they're drinking." Lenora grins.

Before we can move to get drinks, Grady Jackson appears. He kisses Charlotte on top of her head before setting a tray of shots in front of us. "Thanks, babe." Charlotte tilts her head back to look at him.

"Love you, Charlee," he says, not bothering to lower his voice.

He's gone just as fast as he appeared. Our entire table turns to watch him leave. He's sitting with Tucker, Ryder, Malcolm, and Grayson. My heart rate kicks up at seeing Grayson out. It's not something he often does, and I know it's going to take extreme effort to keep from drooling over him all night. I make a mental note to limit the amount of alcohol I consume. I need to keep my wits about me.

"You're drooling," my sister leans in to whisper.

I wipe at my chin, making her laugh. That's when I realize I'm the only one still staring at their table. My cheeks flame with embarrassment. I grab my shot from the tray, tilting it back.

So much for limiting my alcohol.

"So..." Charlotte grins. "How about we talk about the latest edition of the *MC Scoop?*"

I groan as the table hoots with laughter. Eyeing the tray, I see there is one shot left. I grab it, tilting it back, then slamming it on the table. "Let's not." I grimace. My friends get the hint and leave me alone. I try my best to not look in the direction of the table the guys are sitting at, but it's really difficult. Instead, I keep emptying my glass and refilling it. Over and over again.

It's been a long time since I've been this wasted.

Chapter 9

GRAYSON

THE GIRLS ARE SPENDING THE night with my parents. I was resolved to a night of cleaning the house, getting caught up on laundry, and sleeping in. When Ryder called telling me everyone was getting together at Pony Up, I tried to decline. He wasn't having it. Apparently, he ran into my parents and the girls in town, and they told "Uncle Ryder" they were having a sleepover with Nana and Pop.

So, here I am. Sitting at a table in the back so that Tucker and Grady can keep an eye on their women. Not that I blame them. I did the same thing with my late wife more times than I can count.

"Damn, the Abbott sisters are looking good tonight," Malcolm comments. "When did Lenora get back in town?"

"Today," Tucker answers. We all turn heads to look at him. "What? My girl talks, I listen." He shrugs.

"Pussy." Grady coughs the word into his arm.

"Right." Tucker tosses his head back in a laugh. "Like Charlotte doesn't have your balls in a vise."

Grady grins. "It's fun, right?" he asks.

"Every fucker in this place is watching them," Ryder grumbles.

I look at my best friend, trying to get a read on him. I know he's struggling with the fact that his ex-wife is in the center of the group. Olivia is beautiful, with long blonde hair and blue eyes. Those two have more history than the actual History Channel. He doesn't talk about it, not anymore. They've been separated for a while now. I know he still loves her and that damn bird of theirs. I've tried to tell him to let the petty shit go, but here he sits, still brooding.

I know what it's like to have the love of your life and lose her. Not just in a separation, but to have her no longer walking on this earth. That shit cuts deep, and if I could give any of these guys a piece of advice, it would be to remember that. Life is short, more for some of us than others. Live and love each day as if it could be your last.

"Let them have their fun," I tell him.

He glares at me, but it doesn't faze me. I know he's hurting and stubborn as hell. I've been where he is. I've lived through the pain of losing the woman I loved. I know the hell he's living through, and I wouldn't wish it on my worst enemy.

"That's right, seems like you've staked a claim to Laken." Grady smirks.

"Fucking Tate," I grumble, and the guys all laugh. Thankfully, that's the end of talking about Tate and her damn gossip column. The joys of living in a small town.

"I need another," Tucker says, standing.

"I'll go with you," I tell him, pushing back my chair and standing. I follow him through the crowd and stop to stand next to him at their table as he checks in on Justine.

"Good to see you, Grayson." Justine waves at me.

"You too." I nod. I scan the table and notice Charlotte is staring off in the distance. Following her gaze, I see her eyes are locked on Grady as he talks about something animatedly with Malcolm.

On their own accord, my gaze swings to Laken to find her watching me. "Hi." She raises her hand in an awkward wave.

"Laken," I greet her. Her hazel eyes smile at me, and something happens—I feel a lightness in my chest. Something I haven't felt in years, not since that night.

"Hey, Grayson." Lenora smiles.

"Hey, Leni. Visiting long?" I ask. She moved away after high school.

"Actually, I'm home. Just got back today."

"Really? Well, welcome home." Her facial expression tells me she wants to say something else, but she doesn't.

"Have the girls been working on their story?" Laken asks, her face turning a light shade of pink.

I laugh. "You've created literary monsters," I tell her. "They made sure to tell my parents they had a story for them when I dropped them off earlier tonight."

"They're great kids." She turns to look at Lenora. "They're four, so they would get along with Trace."

"Your son?" I ask Lenora. I knew she had a kid, but that's about the extent of my memory where that's concerned.

"Yeah. He starts kindergarten in the fall."

"My twins are a year behind him."

"We should do a play date."

"Sure." I shrug. "The girls would love that." Lenora nods, and our conversation lulls. I'm trying really hard not to stare at Laken. Her long red hair hangs down her back with a slight wave tonight, and it's sexy. I shake out of my thoughts. It's been a long damn time since a thought in regard to a woman being sexy has crossed my mind. It has to be the way she's good to my girls. It's got me off-kilter.

"Ready?" Tucker asks.

"Yeah. See you, ladies, later." I wave and follow Tucker to the bar.

"Which one?" he asks after ordering the girls' entire table another round of beers, shots, and five bottles of water.

"What do you mean?"

"Which sister is yours?"

"Um... neither of them." I don't know what gave him the idea that either of them was mine. I know he's not a Mason Creek native, but he's been around for a few years now.

"Huh," he says, handing over his credit card to pay.

"What do you mean, huh?"

"Just seemed like there might be some interest there."

"Nope," I say, popping the *p*.

"You sure about that?" he asks, turning his back to the bar, resting his elbows on the ledge.

"Yes."

"Maybe you should tell her that." He gives a subtle nod toward where the girls are sitting. Unable to stop it, I mirror his position, resting my elbows casually on the bar as well, and my eyes connect with hers.

Laken.

She turns away quickly, but I caught her. I didn't get a good read on her facial expression, but it was obvious she was observing me. I watch her as

Justine leans in close, and then her sister does the same from the other side. Laken shakes her head, and I am curious as hell as to what they're talking about.

"Looks like it's the younger sister," Tucker comments.

"Nah. The only females I'm giving attention to these days are my four-year-old daughters."

"As you should be, but let me tell you, brother, she wouldn't want you to be lonely." Before I can utter a rebuttal, he's telling me to pick up one of the two trays of drinks and walks away.

Grabbing the tray of drinks, I follow after him. I make it to the table and pass out the shots, one for each of them. "You ladies have rides home?" I ask them as they reach for their shots.

"This one." Justine smiles at Tucker as he presses a kiss to her cheek before handing her a bottle of water.

"Grady." Charlotte smiles, holding her shot glass up in salute before tossing it back.

"Liv?" I question. She knows what I'm asking without me having to say the words.

"Yeah, Grady and Charlotte are taking me home." She closes her eyes and tilts her head back, taking the shot like a pro.

"Good." I nod. "What about the two of you?" I turn my attention to the Abbott sisters.

"Laken drove," Lenora says as she quickly grabs her shot and tilts it back, just like the others have.

"Laken?"

"Uh... we'll walk." She shrugs, grabs her shot, and shoots it back.

"You girls behave," Tucker says after setting a fresh beer in front of each of them and walking away.

Looking down at my tray that holds two bottles of water, I'm ready to hand them to the girls, but I know they're already too far gone. Even if they switch to water now, there is no way that any of them are driving home.

Over the next few hours, the guys and I shoot the shit, all while keeping an eye on their table. When the clock strikes midnight, I yawn, which makes me feel much older than my thirty years. It's been ages since I've been out this late. Unless it's one of the girls up sick or with a nightmare, I'm usually in bed exhausted by this hour.

"You all right, old man?" Ryder teases.

I chuckle lightly. "I think it's time for me to call it a night."

"Ry?" A feminine voice sounds from behind us. All eyes turn to see Olivia standing behind us.

"You okay?" Ryder is immediately on alert.

"Yeah." She sways on her feet. "Take me home?"

Without a word, Ryder stands, gives us a nod, and slips his arm around her waist, leading her out the door.

"Looks like they're all losing steam." Grady chuckles.

"We better get them home." Tucker stands and stretches before draining his bottle of water.

"What about the other two?" Malcolm asks. He obviously knows that Tucker has Justine, and Grady has Charlotte.

Tucker gives me a pointed look. I glance at Malcolm, and before I know what I'm doing, the words "I've got them" come spewing out. He gives me a curt nod, tells us he'll see us later, and walks away.

"You sure, man?" Grady asks.

"Yeah, I'll take them. They have no business walking back to Laken's at this hour."

"This is Mason Creek," he reminds me.

I give him a look, and he nods. I don't need to tell him that in no way am I having any more tragedies. Not on my watch. Not if I can help it.

I can see them safely home. There is nothing wrong with that. I'm just being neighborly. Hell, I'm a firefighter. It's practically in my job description to help damsels in distress. Granted, they're not in distress, but they are highly intoxicated.

"Laken, Leni," I say, approaching their table. "I was hoping you ladies would let me drive you home."

"Oh!" Justine says. "Laken," she says, getting her friend's attention and wagging her eyebrows. I have to fight back a grin at how ridiculous she looks. Not only that, but with the *MC Scoop*, everyone in town is talking about my new "love" interest. Her friend isn't hiding her approval of the matter.

"W-We can walk," Laken says, turning her attention back to me.

"I know, but I need to stop by the fire station." Lies. "It's on the way." I give her what I hope is a charming smile. It's been a while since I've tried to muster up anything remotely charming.

"Thank you, Grayson." Lenora tries to smile, but it's more of a smirk.

Damn. How much have these ladies had to drink? "You're welcome. You ready?" I ask them.

"I need a hug!" Justine announces.

I watch as Charlotte stumbles out of her chair and, with Grady's help, gives Justine a hug goodbye. Lenora is next, and she's a little steadier on her feet. Finally, it's Laken's turn. She pushes back in her chair and stands. Immediately, she loses her footing, but I swoop in and catch her in my arms. My hands slide to her waist to steady her.

"I-I'm sorry," she says, staring up at me. Her hazel eyes are glassy but still gorgeous.

"Can you stand?" I ask her.

"Yeah."

Reluctantly, I release my hold on her, and she again stumbles. Quickly, I slide my arm around her waist and help her to where Justine is standing with Tucker's help. The girls manage to hug, and then Laken is stumbling again. I pull her closer, and she rests her head on my chest, snuggling close. I ignore what it feels like to have her in my arms. I ignore the way my heart stutters in my chest, and my cock swells in my jeans. I can ignore all of that and pretend like it's no big deal when it's anything but. This is the first woman, besides my late wife, to ever garner this reaction from my body. Since I'm in the habit of ignoring things, I push that out of my mind as well.

"Smell good," she mumbles.

Luckily, the bar's loud, and I'm the only one who heard her. At least, I hope so. That's all either of us needs are more rumors flying about the two of us. This is Mason Creek, after all, and the gossip mill is strong. My eyes scan the room, looking for Tate.

Lenora smiles at us, and this time it's a real smile. She walks to where I stand with her sister in my arms and links her arm through mine. I don't know what's happening right now. I kind of feel like I'm in an alternate universe having both of the Abbott sisters in my arms, well close enough. I have one on each arm, so to speak.

"You good?" Grady asks.

"Yeah." I nod, and, with a mind of its own, my hand holds Laken just a little tighter.

"Call if you need help," Tucker tells me.

"I'll be fine. Ready, ladies?" I ask them.

Laken mumbles, as does Lenora, so I take that as yes. Carefully, one foot in front of the other, we make our way out of the bar and to my truck.

"Where are we headed, ladies?" I ask once I have them both in my truck and buckled in, a feat I wasn't sure I was going to be able to accomplish with all their wiggling around. I thought the twins were bad.

"Uh, I can't go to Mom and Dad's like this," Lenora moans. "Don't want Trace to see me."

I glance in the rearview mirror at Lenora and nod. I know where she's coming from. I assume Trace is her son, and I wouldn't want my daughters to see me in the state that she's in either.

"My house. Do you know where I live, Grayson Davis?" Laken asks, making me smile.

"Yes, Laken Abbott, I know where you live." Did she forget this is Mason Creek?

"Good. That's good," she mumbles, resting her head against the window.

The drive to her place is short. I pull up to the back entrance and park my truck, retrieving the keys. "Home sweet home," I tell them.

"Thanks, Grayson." Lenora manages to unbuckle her belt and push open the back door.

I climb out of the truck and rush around to help her. "I'm good," she assures me. "However, Laken might need some help. She doesn't drink. I don't either, not really, but Laken definitely had more than usual."

"She okay?" I ask her.

"Yeah, there's this guy she's always crushed on that was there. She needed liquid courage, I guess."

She shrugs, and I can't explain why, but a surge of something... almost like jealousy courses through me. It's ridiculous. I have nothing to be jealous about. She's not mine, but the feeling is there all the same.

"She doesn't need it," I mumble. If she needs alcohol to be around this guy, she doesn't need to be with him.

"What's that?" Lenora asks.

"Nothing."

"That—" She points at a sleeping Laken in the passenger seat of my truck. "It's what happens when your high school crush is suddenly in your inner circle."

My mind races as I run through all the men who were at the bar tonight and which one could be her crush. I'm pulled out of my thoughts by Lenora's laugh.

"It's you, Grayson," she says. Reaching around me, she grabs Laken's purse from the floorboard and reaches in, pulling out the keys. "You might have to carry her." With that, she walks to the door, manages to unlock it, and leans against it, holding the door open for us.

It's you, Grayson.

Scrubbing my hands over my face, I sigh. I need to get Laken inside and get my ass home. "Laken." I shake her shoulder. Nothing. She's out. "Laken, you're home," I tell her. This time her eyes flutter open.

A slow sexy smile pulls at her lips. "I like this dream."

I don't know why I do it, but I cradle her cheek in the palm of my hand. "You're not dreaming, babe. Can you walk?"

"This is my dream. You have to carry me."

Shaking my head, trying not to smile, I lift her into my arms and kick the door closed. She snuggles in close, wrapping her arms around my neck. "You feel so real," she murmurs.

"Oh my God." Lenora guffaws. "I'm never going to let her live this down."

Walking past her, I give her a stern look. "Let's just keep this between us, yeah?"

"No way, Davis," she says, calling me by my last name. "I wish I would have recorded it." She grins.

Hitting the stairs, I carry Laken up them with ease and step back, waiting for Lenora to unlock the apartment door. Inside is a small studio-style apartment. I take her to the corner and place her gently on the bed.

"Gray?" Laken asks.

"Yeah?"

"You smell good." With that, she rolls over and closes her eyes.

Unable to stop myself, I brush her red hair out of her eyes and pull the cover over her. When I turn to leave, I see Lenora standing with her arms crossed over her chest, watching me.

"Thanks for the ride, Grayson."

"Between us," I remind her.

She nods. "Not for you, but for her. She'd be devastated."

I want to look back, but I know that I shouldn't. I feel a connection toward Laken, and it's fucking with me. Instead, I tell Lenora goodnight and remind her to lock up after me.

The ride to my place is quick. I walk straight to the cabinet over the refrigerator and grab the bottle of whiskey that I sometimes indulge in. I pour myself a glass and down it before pouring another. I try to drink the beautiful Laken out of my mind, but it's impossible.

Giving up, I clean up the kitchen and the living room, but I'm still amped up. For the first time in three years, I fall asleep thinking of someone other than my late wife, and I'm not sure I know how to handle that.

Chapter 5

LAKEN

"Morning sunshine!" my sister says. I feel the bed dip, and without cracking an eye open, I know she's sitting next to me.

"Too early," I grumble.

"It's ten."

"Too early," I repeat, making her laugh.

"Come on, lazybones. Grab a shower, and we can walk to get your car, and you can take me home."

"How do you not feel like death?" I ask her.

"I didn't drink as much as you did."

"Why not? And why did you let me? This is your fault," I blame her. However, there is no heat in my tone. We both know I'm a big girl and did this all on my own.

"You needed to let loose. You never do."

"Wait, did we walk home last night?" I try to pull up the memories from our night out with the girls at Pony Up. I remember lots of shots, and the guys were there, but they didn't bother us.

"Nope. Grayson gave us a ride."

My arm that's thrown over my eyes falls to my side, and I peel my eyes open, blinking a few times to adjust to the bright light. "Say that again."

"Grayson Davis. He gave us a ride home. You should call him and thank him, make him some cookies or something. He did carry you upstairs." There is a smirk playing on her lips, and I remind myself that I'm glad that she's home.

I sit up. My head pounds, but I need to be looking at her for this conversation. "He did what?" I ask, suddenly not feeling as hungover as before, as panic sets in.

"He carried you upstairs. It was very sweet."

"No. No. No. Oh my God, Leni. I'm never drinking again!" Closing my eyes tight, I fall back against the pillows and try to pull up my foggy memories from last night. I vaguely remember him helping me into his truck.

"What happened?" I ask my sister.

"He helped us both into his truck and out of it. You were passed out, so he carried you. He put you to bed and left."

I swallow hard. "What do you mean? He put me to bed?" Lifting the covers, I look to see what I'm wearing, and I'm in nothing but my shirt and panties. Looking over the edge of the bed, I see my skirt on the floor. My wide eyes find hers, and she chuckles.

"You did that all on your own. He simply laid you in bed, covered you up, and left."

"Perfect," I say sarcastically.

"Come on. It's not that bad. We've all been there."

"Did I do or say anything that I shouldn't have? And for your information. I've never been so drunk that Grayson or any man had to carry me to bed."

"No, you were fine. Come on. Get up and get moving. I need to go see my boy."

"Fine," I grumble. Tossing off the covers, I make my way to the bathroom to shower. As I'm stripping out of my clothes, I think back, and nothing new comes to mind. I wish like hell I could remember. Grayson freaking Davis was in my apartment, and he carried me to bed, and I can't remember. Just my damn luck.

There's a knock on the bathroom door. "Yeah!" I call out, cringing when the sound of my own voice causes my headache to throb even more.

"You might want to take a look at the *MC Scoop*." Lenora chuckles when I groan.

"Damnit, Tate!" I curse.

Wrapping a towel around my body, I go back to my room, grabbing my phone and pulling up the blog.

Pony Up Shenanigans

Buckle up, ladies and gents. Looks like our fire chief and bookstore owner are moving forward with their romance. With the perfect embrace, the lady in question, along with her sister, were escorted home by our handsome chief.

Love is in the air.

Tossing my phone on the bed, I stomp back to the shower. My sister's laughter follows me. Not only did Grayson have to drive my drunk ass home, now he has to deal with this. I need to stop and have a talk with Tate. Not that it will do a damn bit of good. She's relentless in her reporting of Mason Creek gossip.

"You coming inside?" my sister asks when I pull into our parents' driveway after we've collected my car.

"No. I don't need a lecture from Mom. I need to go to the store, and do laundry. If I get in there and start playing with Trace, I'll never get home and get everything done."

"Fine. Trace and I will stop by the store one day this week to see you. I've got some things to figure out, and we need to find our own place, stat."

Leaning over the console, I hug her tight. "I'm so glad you're both home. I've missed you."

"I missed you too, Laken. I'll see you this week." She climbs out of the car and leans down, sticking her head through the window. "Don't forget you owe Grayson some cookies or brownies or something." She winks and rushes away, bounding up the front steps of our parents' house.

I can't even be mad about her teasing. She knows I crushed on Grayson hard in high school, and she also knows the adult me is still freaking out about last night. And well, she's home, where she belongs. I'll take all the teasing she can dish out. I'm just glad she's here to do it in person.

Backing out of the driveway, I turn to go back to town—the destination Mason Creek Market. I might as well get the grocery shopping marked off the list while I'm out.

The drive to the market is short. Grabbing a cart from the parking lot to help out the teenagers who are hired to collect them, I wheel inside, and I'm immediately hit with the gush of cool air from the air conditioning. It definitely makes for a more pleasant shopping experience in relation to the hot summer temperature outside today.

I take my time going up and down each aisle, grabbing items from my list and many that aren't. Turning down the aisle to grab deodorant, I hear a masculine voice that I recognize.

"Girls, sit."

I look up to see Grayson pushing a cart, and as I approach, I see the girls are the only thing inside. "Miss Waken!" They wiggle in the cart and point toward me as I pull my cart next to theirs.

"Ladies." I smile at them.

"Looked what we done." Harlow holds her hands out, and Hayden follows suit. Their hands are covered in nail polish. Their nails are painted, but so are the majority of their fingers.

"Wow!" I exclaim. I chance a look at Grayson, and he doesn't look impressed. "Did Daddy help you with your nails?" I ask them. I know enough about kids to know they're going to out themselves. Which is what I want them to do.

"Nope," they say in unison.

"We done it all," Harlow announces proudly.

I know it's not my place, but Grayson looks to be at his wit's end. Placing my hands on my hips, I look between the two of them. "You know you're not supposed to do things like that without asking Daddy first," I remind them.

"Hims would say no," Hayden replies.

"That's because it's Daddy's job to protect you. Even from the pretty nail polish." I hold out my hand so they can see my painted nails. "See how the color is only on my nails?" They bob their little heads up and down. "That's why Daddy would have said no. It's not good to paint your skin with nail polish." Their little lips jut out, and I feel awful, but it's true.

"We don't know how," Harlow says, her voice quivering.

"Laken?"

I look up to find Grayson watching me intently. I'm ready for him to tell me that I was out of line, and I know that I was, but my heart goes out to all three of them. This man is raising two little girls on his own, and I thought maybe hearing from a woman, they might take my advice a little better. It was wrong, and I owe him an apology.

"I'm sorry," I blurt. "I was out of line. I just thought, well, I'm sorry." I can't find it in me to tell him that I thought a woman's word might help. That's a kick in the gut to him.

"You're fine, Laken. In fact, I appreciate the backup. It's not something I often have."

I want to ask him about his parents or his late wife's parents, but I don't have to.

"Their grandparents, both sets, tend to spoil them. Hence the reason they have nail polish anyway. Apparently, Mom bought it for them. She let them take it home when I picked them up this morning after begging. She claims they promised to not use it until I dropped them back off tomorrow afternoon for my shift. You see how that turned out." He nods toward where the girls are sitting in the cart, looking sad.

"Well," I say, clearing my throat. "Let's see what we can do to get this all cleaned up." I move to step around him and grab a bottle of fingernail polish remover and a bag of cotton swabs. "This should do it," I say, handing it to him.

"Will it work for their skin?" he asks.

"It should. It might take a few attempts. This one doesn't have acetone, which is better for their skin."

"And the back patio?"

"I'm not sure about that." I laugh. "I'd say you could get some acetone and spray it off, but I can't really say."

"Thank you, Laken. You've been a huge help," he says, grabbing three more bottles of nail polish remover and another bag of cotton swabs. I don't tell him that it's overkill. Instead, I let him do his thing.

"I like brownies," Hayden says, pointing to the two brownie mixes in my cart.

"You do? Well, these are for your daddy. He helped my sister and me last night, and this is his thank you." I turn to look at Grayson.

"Not necessary, Laken."

"It's the least I could do."

"Can we help?" Harlow asks.

I look up at Grayson, and I can see the war he's waging with himself. He's very protective of his daughters and who they get close to. "That's up to your dad," I tell the girls.

"Please, Daddy."

"Oh, please," they plead with him.

Grayson rakes his hand through his hair and exhales. "Can we do it at our place? I need to get this polish off them, and well, I just... I don't really...." He hesitates.

"Whatever you're comfortable with. They're your babies, Grayson."

He nods. "Our place works," he says cautiously.

"We don't have to," I say, keeping my voice low for only him to hear.

"No. It's fine. It's just... not something I do. Have women in our home. Other than family, that is."

"I'm sorry. I can just—" I start, but he stops me with his hand on my arm. His touch is like fire against my skin. Fire mixed with an electric shock. He looks at his hand against my skin, and his mouth falls open. Does he feel it too?

Clearing his throat, he replies, "It's fine, Laken. Thank you. They'll love it." I nod. "You know where we live?"

"Yeah." I smile. "This is Mason Creek."

He chuckles. "True."

"Well, I need to finish my shopping, and then I'll be over."

"Yay! Brownies with Miss Waken!" the girls cheer.

I step closer to the cart. "Now, you have to promise me that you'll be good for your daddy. I won't be able to come over if your rooms are messy either. So you better get on that when you get home."

They gasp. "Miss Waken, did you go to our house before?" Harlow asks.

"Daddy, how does she know our room is messy?" Hayden asks.

Grayson and I have to bite down on our lips to keep from laughing. "I'm an adult. I know these things."

"Daddy, we hafta go." Harlow looks at him with wide eyes.

"Go fast, Daddy," Hayden chimes in.

"You've bewitched my children." Grayson chuckles. It's a deep throaty sound that I wish I could hear every single day.

"They're sweet girls." He nods in response. "I'm going to finish up here and run home to unload. Give me an hour or so?"

"That sounds good. Are you sure?"

I look at the girls and smile. "I'm sure, Grayson. I'll see you soon, ladies." I wave to them and push my cart down the aisle. I manage to remember it was deodorant that I needed in this aisle, so I grab some and toss it in the cart. Then I circle back around and pick up eggs and a small bottle of cooking oil for the brownie mix. I already had those things at home, but I'm not baking them at home. Then I decide to pick up some disposable foil pans. I'm sure Grayson has some, but in the event that he doesn't, we'll be covered.

I make it back to where I left off and finish the last few rows of my shopping before pushing the cart to the checkout.

As I wait my turn, I can't help but smile. I've lived in this town with Grayson Davis my entire life, and in the last week, I've had more interactions with him than I would have in an entire year. I'm excited to spend time with the three of them, but I have to remember to remind myself that I'm there to help bake some thank-you brownies with his daughters. I'm not there for the man.

Chapter 6

GRAYSON

A S SOON AS WE PULL into the driveway, the girls are unbuckling from their car seats and literally bouncing at the thought of Laken coming to make brownies with them.

"Wait until the truck is off before you open the door," I remind them.

"Hurry, Daddy!" they exclaim in harmony.

I slow to a crawl just to mess with them. "Daddy," Harlow whines.

"Faster!" Hayden demands.

I can't help but laugh as I park my truck and turn off the engine. They move to the door and start to climb out. "Wait for me," I tell them. Reaching in, I hit the garage door opener before closing my door. My truck is too long to fit, but going into the house through the garage keeps the house cleaner. The girls know to kick off their shoes in the laundry room, and that door stays unlocked, so if someone has to potty, we can race inside quickly without incident. I learned that one the messy way. After a few accidents, you learn to make adjustments.

"We're big girls, Daddy. We're this many." Harlow raises four fingers in the air.

"Yeah," Hayden echoes.

Biting my cheek to hide my smile, I lift them from the truck, and they take off, sprinting for the front door. "Where are you going? We have nail polish to tend to," I call after them.

"We hafta cwean our room!" one of them yells back. Is it bad that they also sound so much alike that sometimes even I can't tell them apart unless they are right in front of me?

Grabbing the bag of cotton swabs and fingernail polish remover, I head into the house. I opt to leave the garage door open. Laken will be here in the next hour or so, and it's going to be hard to keep the girls contained. I'll be able to keep them in the garage until Laken is parked. After that, all bets are off.

Placing the bag on the kitchen counter, I take a look at the house. The kitchen is clean, and the living room is picked up. I did it all last night when I got home and was too amped up to sleep. It felt good to hold Laken in my arms, even if I was just carrying her up to her apartment. It's been just over three years since I've held a woman in my arms. It's been the same amount of time since I've been with a woman.

It's not because I'm harboring some sort of faithfulness to my late wife. I know that Holly is gone, and I know she would want me to move on. I'd like to think I will someday. However, right now, raising twin girls on my own and being promoted to fire chief, well, that doesn't leave a lot of time left for dating.

Not only that, but this is Mason Creek, and everyone knows everyone. I already have the old ladies in town trying to fix me up with their granddaughters. Many of which are way too damn young for me. I just haven't felt like bringing someone around the girls was a good thing. They're young and so damn impressionable and full of questions.

I'm just not ready.

Yet, I still told Laken she could come over. Part of me didn't want to disappoint my daughters. There's an even bigger part that wanted to spend some time with her. My girls will be there, and they already know her. They adore her, if the last week has shown me anything. It's not a big deal. Just being neighborly and all that.

My phone rings, pulling me out of my thoughts. "Hey," I greet Ryder. "How's Olivia?"

"Pissed that she asked me to take her home last night."

"Did you stay the night?"

"Yeah," he sighs. "Fuck, man. I couldn't leave her there alone that drunk. What if she needed something?"

I don't answer, and I know he doesn't really want me to. Ryder and Olivia love one another, but they're both too busy getting in their own way. "That's tough, man."

"That it is. What are you and the girls getting into tonight? I thought about swinging by."

"We're uh… shit," I mutter. "The girls are making brownies."

"You don't bake."

"Nope."

"Your mom or Christine?" he asks.

"Neither." I should have just let his call go to voice mail.

"So the twins are just going to learn how to bake on their own?"

"No."

"Come on, man, help me out here. What's going on?"

"Fine," I concede. "I might have run into Laken at the market. And somehow, it ended up with the girls helping her make brownies. Brownies that were intended for me as a thank-you for getting her and Leni home last night."

He whistles, and that alone pisses me off and makes me wish I would have just kept my mouth shut. "So, what? Laken's coming over?"

"She is."

"When?"

"Within the hour."

He's quiet for several long seconds that feel like a lifetime. "You doing okay?"

His question catches me off guard. "Yeah, of course, why wouldn't I be?"

"Come on, Gray. This is the first woman you've had around the girls intentionally, and she's coming to your house. That's a big fucking deal."

"It's not," I lie. "It's her being nice to the girls. Mom takes them to her bookstore once a week, and they've grown fond of her. They asked her if they could help when they saw brownies in her cart, and she volleyed the answer to me. I couldn't tell them no."

"You're their father. It's your job to tell them no."

"They don't get to do these types of things. At least not unless it's with my mom or Holly's." What I don't say is that they don't have their mom here to do these kinds of things with. And while my mom and Holly's do so much for them, I have a feeling baking with Laken will be a completely different experience.

"All right, you know what you're doing. At least I hope that you do."

"Not even a little bit," I confess, making him laugh.

"All right, well, call me later. I'm gonna need to hear how it goes."

"Yeah, yeah," I mutter. "I need to go check on the girls. They're being really quiet, and they're cleaning their room, so that usually means trouble."

"How'd you con them into cleaning their room?" He's obviously heard me complain about the mess my two angels make of their room. Mostly with clothes.

"That's just it. I didn't. Laken made a comment about being good and keeping their room clean so that she could come over. As soon as we pulled in, they ran to their room like their little asses were on fire. They're afraid if it's not clean, she won't stay and bake with them."

"Wow. Good motivation. Maybe you should make this a weekly thing? You know, Laken coming to visit."

"You let me worry about me and my... visitors. You have enough on your plate." It's a dick move, and I regret it instantly. "Sorry, man. I'm out of my element here."

"I get it. And you're right. If my wife wasn't so damn stubborn—" I can hear the frustration in his voice, which isn't anything new, not when it comes to Ryder and Olivia.

"I feel for you, but I'm telling you sometimes you have to choose your battles. You love her, and she loves you. You two need to get past whatever it is and make it right." This isn't the first time I've given him this speech. I'm sure it won't be the last.

"Call me later?"

"If I survive." I chuckle.

"Oh, I have a feeling you're going to more than survive. I'll catch you later." He ends the call before I can ask what he meant by that comment. I start to call him back and remember I need to check on the girls.

Sliding my phone into my back pocket, I make my way down the hall to the girls' bedroom. Peeking inside the door, I see that the mess of clothes is somewhat cleaned up if you could call being shoved into dresser drawers and clothes baskets tidy. It's clean for four year olds, that's for sure.

"What's going on?" I ask.

They both jump and stop to turn and look at me. "We need help," Harlow huffs, pulling on her comforter.

"I think we need to be this many," Hayden holds up her hand, displaying all five fingers, "to make beds." She lets the top half of her body fall dramatically on the bed with a groan.

"You can't give up," I tell her. "You'll never learn if you stop trying."

"But I'm too wittle," she huffs.

"Yeah, Daddy. We're too wittle," Harlow agrees.

"Life is not always easy. You have to keep pushing and working hard. No matter what you're doing." I'm trying to bestow some fatherly wisdom on them at their impressionable young age. Hell, if I know if it's working.

"Yeah, but Miss Waken is coming, and if ours rooms not cwean, she might not cook the brownies," Hayden argues.

"We weally wove bwonies, Daddy," Harlow adds.

Bending my knees, I hold my arms out, and neither of them hesitates to come to me, wrapping their little arms around my neck. My heart swells just like it does every time I get even the smallest embrace from them. "Daddy has a secret."

"We won't tell," Hayden assures me.

"We pwomise," Harlow adds.

"Daddy loves brownies."

They gasp. "Does Miss Waken wove them too?" Harlow asks.

"I don't know, baby. I'm sure she does. Who doesn't love brownies?"

"We hafta ask her," Hayden announces.

"We can do that when she gets here. Right now, I need you to help me make your beds." That's all it takes for them to rush off to their respective bed and wait for me to help them make it. It ends up being all three of us making each bed because, if anything, my girls love to help. We're just finishing placing Harlow's stuffed animals on hers when there's a knock at the door.

"It's her!" they say in harmony and rush out of their room and down the hall.

"Wait for me!" I call after them.

When I reach the living room, Laken is standing at the door and giving my girls a stern look. "Did I not hear your daddy yelling for you to wait for him?" she asks them.

"But you's not a stwanger, Miss Waken."

"I might not be a stranger, but you never answer the door on your own. You never know who is going to be standing on the other side. It's important that when your daddy makes rules that you listen to him."

She's so good with them. I'm sure I should be upset that she's counseling my daughters, but they look up to her. That's easy to see. If her little speech helps keep them safe, then I'm all for it.

"Sowwy," they say at the same time.

"Hey," I say, walking the rest of the way into the room. "Come on in." The girls take that as their cue to push open the door for Laken to enter our home. This is the only home they ever remember living in. I sold the house that Holly and I were having built the minute that it was finished. I just couldn't bring it in me to live there without her. Instead, I found this place on the market. It had been fully renovated and was more than enough space for me and the girls. We packed up our rental and moved in a few weeks later. Laken is officially the first woman to ever step inside who's not related to my daughters or me.

"Are you ladies ready to make some brownies?" Laken holds up a bag full of supplies.

"So weady!" the girls cheer.

"All right then, lead the way to the kitchen."

Jumping into action, I reach out and take the bag from her hands. "Thanks, Grayson," she says softly before taking a hand of each of my daughters and letting them drag her to the kitchen.

I follow along behind them with the bag of supplies, doing my best not to watch her ass sway in those leggings she has on. I'm not sure who invented the first pair of leggings, but I can almost guarantee it was a man.

In the kitchen, I place the bag on the island as the girls climb up onto the stools. I keep them steady to make sure they don't tip over.

"Okay, first things first. You can call me Laken. Miss Laken is very formal, and all of my closest friends call me Laken." She smiles at my daughters.

"Waken," they repeat.

"Perfect. Now. I'm going to need your daddy to help me out with the bowls and spoons and a measuring cup?" she asks, glancing up at me.

With that one look, something happens to me. There's a flutter in my chest, and my cock twitches. It's been over three years since I've felt attraction, and my cock decides that now, standing in my kitchen with my four-year-old twin daughters, is the best time to get back in the game.

"Grayson?" Laken asks.

I realize I've just been standing here staring at her. "Right." I jump into action, showing her where everything is. "Just let me know if there is something else you might need."

"I think we're good. If you have something to do, yard work or laundry or whatever, we'll be fine," she assures me.

"Thanks. I might take you up on that." There's always something that needs to be done.

"No! Daddy, you hafta make dem wif us," Hayden tells me.

"Yeah. You hafta help. What if we can't weach?" Harlow asks.

Laken and I both smile at that one. "My mom always has me reach into the taller cabinets when I'm at my parents' place. It never fails," I explain to Laken.

"Well, then you better stick around." Her smile lights up her face, and that same feeling in my chest makes itself known.

I should walk away. I could mow the lawn, or hell, do some weeding. It's been over a week, and the yard is getting out of control.

I do neither.

Instead, I pull out another stool at the island and watch as Laken takes over my kitchen.

Chapter 7

LAKEN

I KEEP MY ATTENTION ON the twins. I have to. If I let myself think about him, well, let's just say we might burn the brownies.

"Ready, ladies?" I ask the girls.

"Weady!" they cheer. The smile that graces both of their faces warms my heart. They are such sweet little girls. My heart breaks for them with the loss of their mother. Grayson has done a fantastic job raising them. I make a mental note to mention that to him.

"Okay. Well, the first step of baking. You must read the directions, so you know what to expect." I turn one of the two boxes of brownies over and begin to read the directions out loud.

"Waken, we can't wead," Harlow reminds me.

"Well, it's a good thing you have your daddy and me here to help." Harlow nods, satisfied with my answer.

"Okay, so the first step is to preheat the oven. That means that we turn it to the correct temperature and let it warm up before we put the brownies inside. Remember you should never ever touch the stove for any reason unless an adult is standing right beside you." I give them both a look that I would imagine will be what my mom face will be when I someday have children of my own.

"Before we move on, I need for you both to promise me."

"I pwomise," Hayden is quick to reply.

"I pwomise too," Harlow agrees.

"Good." I turn my back to them to preheat the oven before turning back to face them. "All right, ladies. We have two batches, which means that you both get to make your own batch."

"Yay!" Cheers all around make me smile.

"Let's wash our hands, and we'll get started."

"We gots a stool," Hayden says, pulling a small wooden stool with a handle up to the sink.

"That's pretty cool," I tell her.

"Pop made it for us."

"Well, that was very nice of him."

"We gots one in the bafroom too," Harlow chimes in.

I help both of them wash their hands, and they immediately scurry back to their seats at the island.

"Daddy, you hafta wash you hands," Hayden says.

"Daddy's just going to watch, sweetie," Grayson replies, popping her on the nose.

"Waken, tell hims he needs to wash hims hands," Harlow instructs.

"You heard the ladies." I nod toward the sink. The smile he gives me turns me inside out.

"Fine. Three against one. I'm outnumbered. Maybe I should call Ryder to come balance out the male-to-female ratio," he quips.

"Oh, we love Uncle Wyder," the girls say in agreement.

I can't help but laugh. "Okay, ladies. You each get a bowl," I say, directing their attention back to me. Over the next hour or so, we manage to finally get the batter mixed up, minus eggshells. Luckily I had them crack the eggs into a small bowl so we could fish out any shells before dumping them into the batter. There's batter on the counter and on their faces, but that doesn't take away from their smile.

"Now what?" Harlow asks.

"Now, we pour the batter into the pan and place them in the oven. They have to bake for thirty-five minutes."

"That's a wong time." Hayden's eyes are wide.

"Not too long."

"Girls, let's go get you washed up while Laken bakes the brownies."

"Okay, Daddy," they agree.

"Laken, make yourself at home. I'll be back to help you clean up."

"Oh..." I wave him off. "I've got it. It won't take me long at all. Girls, thank you so much for your help. I couldn't have done this without you."

"We're good helpers!" Harlow exclaims.

"You are very good helpers."

Grayson nods, and with one girl on each side holding his hand, he leads them down the hall to what I assume is the bathroom to get them cleaned up. I hear giggles floating down the hall as I wash the dishes, and I don't need to look into a mirror to know I'm smiling. The happiness of those two little girls is infectious.

"I told you I would do that," Grayson says from behind me.

I turn to look at him over my shoulder. He's standing against the island, his arms crossed over his chest. I crushed on the teenage Grayson, and let's just say age has been good to him. He's even more gorgeous than he was way back then. "I don't mind," I reply, quickly turning back to the sink.

I feel him next to me, and a glance out of the corner of my eye confirms it. "I'll dry," he says, taking a bowl from my hands and drying it with a dishtowel.

"Thanks. Where are the girls?"

"Double-checking their room." He smiles and shakes his head. "I've never seen them clean so fast in my life."

"Are they messy?"

"They're four-year-old girls; yeah, they're messy." He chuckles.

"What? Four-year-old boys wouldn't be messy?"

"Don't know." He shrugs. "I can't talk about raising boys. I know that those two can tear up that room faster than I can blink an eye."

"My nephew is five. To hear Leni tell it, he can do the same." We're quiet as I wash the final bowl and hand it to him. I reach for another towel to dry my hands and turn to face him. "They're incredible little ladies, Grayson. You're doing a great job with them."

He nods. I watch as his throat bobs as he swallows. "Some days I wonder."

"Well, don't let today be one of them. They're thriving and happy. You did that." I place my hand on his arm, and I feel a jolt. My eyes immediately seek out his, and he's looking at where I'm touching him. "Sorry," I say and go to move away.

His hand covers mine before I can. "Thank you for today, Laken. Truly. The girls, they have my mom and—" He swallows hard. "—Holly's, but there have been no women around their mom's age in their lives. They're taken with you, and you're so good with them. I know you probably have better things to do than make brownies with my girls, but I'm grateful you did this for them."

"It was my pleasure. I was making them anyway."

"Yeah, but you could have done it a lot faster and cleaner." The corner of his mouth lifts in a grin.

"Maybe, but it's more about the memories." The words are barely out of my mouth when the girls come racing into the kitchen. They don't stop until they both have themselves wrapped around my legs like little monkeys.

"Waken, our woom is cwean," The twin on my left smiles up at me. I think it's Hayden. I still have trouble when they are this close. I can't tell when they're both this excited and from this angle, I can't tell who is taller, which is my other tell at distinguishing which twin is talking.

"I'm so proud of you," I praise them.

"Come see." The twin on my right slides her hand in mine, her sister doing the same, and they pull me down the hall.

"Easy, girls!" Grayson calls out.

"They're fine." I chuckle as we stop at what I assume is their bedroom door. They lead me to a twin bed and tell me to sit, so I oblige. The next fifteen minutes are a flutter of showing me what feels like every toy that they own.

"Ladies, I think we need to check on our brownies."

"Okay."

"How about I go check on them while you put all of this away?" I suggest, looking at items strung out all over the floor.

"Okay," they say again.

Standing from the bed, I head back to the kitchen. Grayson is sitting at the island, scrolling through his phone. "You were right," I tell him. I walk around him to the stove, pulling down the door to check the progress of our brownies.

"Oh, yeah?" he asks, placing his phone on the island.

"They had to show me their toys, and their room is destroyed."

He nods, a smile playing on his lips. "That sounds like my girls."

"I wish I had their energy."

"Right?" he agrees. "Some days, it takes all I have in me to keep up with them. I know my mom and Christine have to be exhausted after keeping them all day."

"I'm sure, but I'm also sure they love every minute of it."

"They do."

"It's nice that you didn't have to put them in daycare. My sister had to put Trace in daycare, and she hated it. I'm glad Mom and Dad will be able to help her out now that they're home."

"Is she home to stay?"

"Yes. At least I hope that they are. It feels like Trace has grown up overnight. I'm excited to get to spoil my nephew more than on visits every few months."

"They do grow up fast," he comments.

Conversation lulls, so I turn to check the brownies again, and they're ready to come out of the oven. I'm removing the second pan when the girls come back into the kitchen.

"Can we have some?" Harlow asks.

"Not yet. They need to cool. How about you slide up on the stool, and I'll help Daddy with this nail polish crisis," I say, pointing at her hands.

"You don't have to," Grayson says.

"I don't mind. That is if you want the help."

"Four hands are better than two." He stands and disappears, only to reappear with the fingernail polish remover and cotton swabs.

"I want nails wike yours," Hayden says.

"Well, I think we might be able to arrange that. As long as it's okay with your dad."

"Oh, can we, Daddy? Pwease?" they say at the same time.

He smiles at them. "As long as Laken has the time."

"I can make the time for my favorite little ladies." I wink at the girls, and they dissolve into a fit of giggles.

"I should probably get going." I stand and toss my napkin from my brownie into the trash. After Grayson and I got the polish off the girls' hands and nails, I repainted their nails, much to their delight. They made sure to point out that I did a better job than their dad, and that he doesn't do it very often. Then they proceeded to tell me that he put all their polish away when they accidentally got into it. But they weren't mad at him because Nana bought them more. The image of Grayson painting his daughters' nails is like a string wrapped around my heart and these two littles and their daddy are tugging on it.

"No," the twins whine.

They're tired, and I'm sure it's getting close to their bedtime. "I have chores to do, like clean my room," I tell them, and they gasp.

"Girls, what do you say?" Grayson asks them.

"Thank you, Waken," they say together. They slide off their stool and rush toward me, each embracing a leg. I bend down and give them true hugs.

"Thank you so much for all of your help today. Can you do me a big favor?"

"Yes."

"We can."

"Make sure you remind your daddy to take these to the firehouse so he can share with his friends."

"But we wants dem," Hayden replies.

"I made a small plate for the three of you, and the rest for Daddy to take to work."

"Yous the best, Waken." Harlow throws her little arms around my neck, almost knocking me back on my ass as she embraces me tightly.

"Sissy's wight," Hayden agrees, and that's when I feel her little arms hugging me too.

Hot tears prick my eyes. These girls have so much love to give, and my heart breaks for them, for Grayson, and for Holly. More than anything, I wish she could be here to see that her daughters have her same kind heart.

"I'll see you, ladies, later this week." I wave and head for the door.

"Girls, go grab some pjs, and I'll be in for a bath in a few minutes. Don't start the water without me," he tells them.

"Okay, Daddy," they reply as their little feet pitter-patter down the hall against the hardwood floor.

Just as I'm about to open the door to leave, Grayson's voice stops me. "Laken." I turn to look at him. "Thank you for today. You made two little girls very happy."

"It was my pleasure."

"Be safe driving home."

"Always." With a wave, I turn the knob and exit their home.

My feet feel as though they are filled with lead as I make my way to my car. I never could have imagined I'd spend a Sunday afternoon with Grayson Davis and his adorable twin daughters.

Now that I have, it's something I want to do all the time. I hate that I'm leaving their home.

That's exactly what it is. It's more than a house. Grayson has made a beautiful home for his daughters.

Me? I live above my business, in a studio apartment. This afternoon has reminded me that I want a family. I want a partner to go through life with, and I want kids. Hell, I even want the dog and the white picket fence.

I got lost in owning and running my business and forgot what life is really about. The memories and the relationships. I think about the hugs given to me and smile.

Life is about the perfect embrace.

Chapter 8

GRAYSON

I WOKE TO ANOTHER ARTICLE about Laken and me. I understand how Tate found out about our run-in at the market. I'm sure she has eyes all over this town willing to give her information for her column. What I don't know is how she found out that Laken came to my place? Not only that, but she knew my girls were there. Her article yammered on about me and my girls getting close to the bookstore owner.

She's not wrong. My daughters are enamored with Laken.

And me? Well, I don't know what I am.

I know I think about her all the time. She's been thrust into my life, and it's as if the universe is trying to show me how great we could be together.

Shaking out of my thoughts, I park my truck behind the firehouse, and my eyes, with a mind of their own, look across the street at One More Chapter. Laken is walking inside the front door with a box from the bakery in her hands. I watch her until she disappears inside.

"Hey, Cap," Jacob says as I walk into the firehouse. He's way too chipper for Monday morning. "Whatcha got there?" He points to the large plastic container in my hands.

"The girls made brownies yesterday." I shrug, walking past him to the small kitchen and placing the container on the table.

"Don't hide behind your daughters. You know you were getting your Betty Crocker on," he teases, opening the container and grabbing a brownie. He shoves half of it into his mouth and moans. "So good," he says once he swallows. "You know, if this Captain thing isn't working for you, maybe you could get a job at the bakery in town," he jokes.

"Laugh it up," I tell him. "See if I bring you in any more snacks."

He shoves the other half of the brownie into his mouth and reaches inside the container for another. "I better enjoy it while I can," he says after swallowing.

I don't need him to tell me how good they are. I had three last night. I also caved and let the girls have them for breakfast. Not my finest moment, but it is what it is. I also don't need to tell him that it wasn't me who helped the girls make the brownies. If they knew that Laken was at my place, baking with my daughters, spending time with them, with us, they'd never let me live it down.

Disappearing into my office to get some paperwork done, I try to push Laken out of my mind. I've lived in the same town as her for my entire life, and now all of a sudden, in the last two weeks, she's everywhere. My daughters adore her, and have for a while now. Laken is the reason for their love of books, and for the fact that my kitchen smells like brownies and her sweet perfume.

I barely slept a wink last night trying to work this... Hell, I don't even know how to explain. The best way I can describe it is desire. My heart races when she's near, and my cock, well, he's definitely ready to party.

I've been hit on countless times since losing my wife, and I've never had this reaction to any of those women. Hell, I've seen Laken since then. I've passed her in the mornings as we both jog around town. I've seen her at the market, and I'm sure a million other instances in the last three years.

Why her? Why now?

I don't have the answers to either of those questions.

Shaking out of my thoughts, I force myself to get busy and forget about my new distraction that is Laken Abbott.

I'm just finishing up our call report for the month when I hear the sounds of my daughters. Yes, I know it's my girls. I would recognize their giggles and little voices anywhere. Mom has them today, and usually, they visit on Thursdays when she takes them to the bookstore. I don't know why they're here, but I'll never pass up a hug from my girls.

Walking out of my office, I see Mom standing with the twins, Jacob, and a few of the other volunteers. Mason Creek is a small town, and we can't afford to pay around the clock full-time firefighters. That makes us mostly volunteer-based. We have some incredible men and women on our crew, and I'm thankful for each and every one of them. They make my job easy, most days. "What? No hug for your dad?" I call out.

The girls turn to look at me and take off running. I bend down and scoop them up in my arms. They're almost too big for me to do this with both of them at the same time. "What are you doing here?"

"We hafta see if the boys wiked the bwonies," Harlow tells me.

"Hey, Mom," I say, walking with the girls, one in each arm to greet her.

"Having a good day?" she asks.

"I am. Better now," I say, kissing each of the twins on the cheek.

"I had to run to the market, and the girls wanted to stop in for a few," she further explains.

"Daddy, we hafta to have Waken make more bwonies. Hims said dey are all gone," Hayden announces.

"Laken?" Jacob asks. "I thought the three of you made the brownies?" he asks, a smirk playing on his lips.

"We made dhem wif Waken and Daddy," Harlow answers.

"Interesting. Does Laken make brownies with Daddy all the time?" Mark, another volunteer, asks.

"Nope," Hayden replies. She then places her hands on my cheeks and turns my head to face her. "Can Waken come make more bwonies?"

"We'll see," I tell her. I don't want to crush her dreams in front of the guys. There might also be a small part of me that wants Laken to come back over and make brownies as well.

"Girls, we should go and let the guys get back to work. We were just stopping in to say hello."

"Be good for Nana," I tell my girls. After a kiss and a hug from both of them, I set them back on their feet, and they immediately go to my mom, each taking one of her hands.

"Laken, huh?" Jacob asks.

"Wait. Hold up. Laken as in One More Chapter? That Laken? The fuck-hot redhead?" Canaan asks.

He knows damn well who we're talking about. Mason Creek is a small town, and he's lived here his entire life.

"That's the one." Mark smirks.

"Don't you all have something to do?"

"Yep. And we're doing it," Jacob remarks.

"Fine. Mom takes the girls to her bookstore once a week. They've grown fond of her. I ran into her at the grocery store, and she had brownies in her cart, and the girls asked to help. You know I'm not about to let them go with her, so she offered to make them at our place, and the girls were so excited, I couldn't say no."

"You don't know how bad I want to give you shit about this." Canaan grins, his eyes twinkling with mischief. "And I plan to, but first, let me just say this." He locks his gaze on mine, suddenly serious, and I know whatever it is he has to say is going to hit deep. That's just how Canaan is. "I can see that this is eating you up inside. Don't let it. You have to live, Grayson. For you, and for those adorable little girls. They need to see what it means for a man to adore a woman. They need to know not to settle for some douchebag who doesn't treat them right. Sure, they can see that with how you treat them, but that's a father's love. They need to see the right way for a man to love a woman."

"Damn, C." Mark whistles.

"*He* has spoken."

I run my hands through my hair. I'm frustrated for these feelings for Laken that I can't explain. Except, if I'm really honest with myself, I know what they are. It's desire. And if I'm truly honest, it feels damn good to feel something again when it comes to a woman.

"I know I'm a flirt, and I play the field, but you can bet your ass if, and when, a woman comes along who I like well enough to let into my home and bake with my daughters, I'm going to pursue her. Pursue that connection and see where it goes," Canaan adds.

"And what happens when she breaks their hearts? Huh? What happens when I let her in, and we lose her?" The words are out of my mouth before I can stop them. I see the sympathy on their faces, and I have no doubt they're all thinking about my late wife.

"What happened to Holly was tragic." I hear from behind me. Turning to look over my shoulder, I see my best friend, Ryder. "It was an accident, Grayson. You can't live your life thinking you're going to lose everyone you get close to. You don't want your daughters to grow up with that worry in the back of their mind. It's your job to show them how to live."

"What is this, tear Grayson apart day?"

"You know that's not what this is." Ryder's tone is scolding.

"We just want to see you happy, Cap," Jacob adds.

"What are you doing here?" I ask Ryder, ignoring Jacob's comment. Do they think I don't miss the feel of a warm body next to mine? That I don't crave the intimacy? When I'm in bed at night that the memories of my late wife and all that she's missing doesn't kill me? All that our daughters are missing? It fucking destroys me.

"Wanted to see if you and the girls wanted to come to dinner at my place tonight. The condo is too damn quiet."

"Olivia have Kiwi this week?" I ask him. Kiwi is their pet bird that they share custody of.

"Yeah," he sighs.

"What can we bring?" I ask him.

"Nothing. I've got it covered. The twins still like those fruit punch drink pouches?"

I nod. "They do."

"Seven. I'll let you get back to saving lives and all that." He smiles and waves before turning and walking away.

"I've got work to do," I mumble, turning on my heel and heading for my office. I've had all of the interventions I can take for one day.

Once I reach my office, I shut the door and lean against it. I know what they're saying is right, but it's not that easy. Hell, I don't even know how to date. Not really.

Holly and I started dating in high school. She's the only woman I've ever slept with. How do I do that? How do I allow myself to sleep with someone else when it was supposed to only have been her? How do I bring another woman into my daughters' lives and still make sure they know who their mother was and that she loved them with every ounce of her soul?

Releasing a sigh, I move to my desk and get back to work. I'm not going to figure it out today. I'm not sure I'll ever figure it out at all.

"Daddy, can we go pway?" Hayden asks.

I look at their mostly empty plates and nod. "Stay where I can see you."

"Okay!" my girls reply, pushing back from the patio table before racing to Ryder's backyard. They go directly for the bag of toys we brought over.

"So, Laken?" Ryder asks as soon as my daughters are out of earshot. "What's going on, man?"

"Fuck if I know." I drain my root beer, wishing it was a real beer. "All of a sudden, she's everywhere. My girls talk about her all that time. I mean, they've mentioned her before, but the last two weeks, it's been Laken this and Laken that. Hell, even my mom and Christine are enamored with her.

"Then the other night, I took her and Lenora back to her place. They were too far gone to drive, and it didn't feel right to let them walk in their condition. I had to carry her upstairs, and when I put her to bed, she told me I smelled good."

"Oh, the horror," Ryder jokes.

"It's the way it made me feel that's horrible."

"How did it make you feel?"

"You sound like a therapist." I laugh.

"Just call me Dr. King." He smirks. "Now, please proceed. We can go inside, and you can lie down on the couch if you'd be more comfortable," he jests.

"Fuck off," I say with no heat in my words. We're both quiet for a few minutes as I stare down at my lap. I hate talking about this shit, but Ryder's my best friend. He was there for me when Holly died, and I've been there for him since his split with his wife, Olivia. This is what we do, even though I hate it.

"Wanted," I finally say. "It's been a long damn time since I've felt that from a woman who's not related to me." I feel wanted by my daughters every day, but this is a different kind of want. It's filled with desire and need and a craving for intimacy.

"She's not just trying to latch on to you so she can say she bagged the elusive bachelor of Mason Creek." He nods in understanding.

"Exactly. Lenora told me she crushed on me all through high school. She also made it sound like she still harbored those feelings. Laken was drunk when she told me that I smelled good. Surely Lenora is mistaken. I can't stop thinking about it. Add in the fact she's all my girls talk about and that she baked with them. And she was there for them, man. She barely paid me any attention. She was so damn patient with them and explained things, but at the same time, she's not a pushover either. It's like she gives them discipline in a way that they don't even realize. She got them to clean their room, and it's stayed clean so far. It's only been a day..." I chuckle. "But those little tornadoes usually don't keep it clean that long."

"For what it's worth, I think you're ready."

"What about them?" I nod toward the small backyard area where the girls are playing. I won't deny that I crave intimacy and companionship. I know Holly would want me to move on and be happy. However, I can't bring just anyone into my daughters' lives.

You already did.

"They'll follow your lead. You can't protect them from heartbreak, Grayson. It's a part of life. It's how you deal with heartbreak. Show them that you have to dust yourself off and try again. Who knows, it might turn into your second chance at happily ever after." It feels like a vise is squeezing my heart in my chest for multiple reasons. One, loving someone who isn't my wife has me feeling all kinds of guilty, and two, the thought of loving Laken, well, that's not a completely unwelcome thought.

"What about you and Olivia?"

"I love her." It's his turn to be in the hot seat. "I don't know if we can salvage our marriage, but I know that I'll always love her."

"I'll always love Holly."

"I get that, man. Any woman in your life from here on out will need to accept that. She gave you those two angels. But you see, our situations are different. Holly is gone. She didn't choose to leave you, Gray. She died, man. I know that's harsh, but it's the facts. You have the chance to move on. My wife left me, and I have to see her around town and drive her drunk ass home from Pony Up. I'll have to watch her move on, and I'm telling you, man, I don't know that I'll be able to handle that."

"Then fight for her."

He nods. "You fight for you. And I'll fight for me."

"I'm not sure I'm ready."

"You are. You just have to admit it to yourself and allow yourself to move on. Holly would want you to move on."

I nod. I've had enough of the deep conversations for the day. I'm at my max capacity for talking about it. "Girls, pack up your toys and give Uncle Ryder a hug. We need to get home and get baths," I call out to my daughters. I watch as they scurry to place everything back in the bag of toys and then rush to hug Ryder.

"Thanks for dinner." I stand and toss our empty plates in the trash.

"Thanks for the company. Leave all that. I'll get it. You've got dad duties."

"You sure?"

"Go." He waves me off.

Grabbing the bag of toys and slinging it over my shoulder, I hold a hand out for each of my girls and lead them to my truck. My conversation with the guys and Ryder earlier today and my conversation with Ryder tonight are replaying in my mind. They've made some good points, and I can admit to myself that I'm lonely. I have my daughters, but I miss the touch of a woman.

I need to get the girls in bed and a shower myself and bed. All of this "feelings" talk has me exhausted.

Chapter 9

LAKEN

"LAKEN! ARE YOU LISTENING TO me?" Lenora asks.

"Uh-huh." My phone is pressed to my ear as I stare out the window.

"Wait. Are they washing the trucks again?" She chuckles.

"It's a hardship, really," I tell her. "To live so close to the firehouse. I mean, watching gorgeous, ripped men wash the trucks every week is a huge distraction."

Her loud, raucous laughter makes me smile. "I think I should stop by and finish this conversation in person. You know, so I can watch the show with you."

"I mean, I've got good seats," I reply while gazing out my window, watching the show as she so eloquently put it. "I could pop us some popcorn."

"Anyway," she says with a chuckle, "get your ass moving. We have appointments at the salon to get our nails done."

"Since when?" I ask, forcing myself to look away from the scenery out my window.

"Since I called and made us one. We have to be there in twenty, so get moving."

"You know I'm going to miss the ending of my show, right?" I say, barely able to contain my laughter.

"You've seen that show once a week or more since you moved in. I think you'll survive."

"Fine. The sacrifices I make for you."

"Hush." She sniggers. "I'll see you in a few. And don't say you have to work. I know you close at one on Saturdays."

"I'm thinking about staying open later. Jasmine mentioned she could use more hours." Jasmine is a senior in high school and a great kid. She's good with the customers, and she loves all books. She reminds me of myself when I was her age.

"Well, we can talk about that when you meet me at the salon."

"Fine. You owe me one."

Her reply is to laugh and hang up on me. My reflection in the mirror shows that my smile is wide, and it has nothing to do with the shirtless men who are currently washing the fire trucks. Don't get me wrong, that's definitely worth smiling about, but this one is for my sister. I'm so damn happy to have her home.

"There she is." Lenora waves at me as I enter the salon. She's already sitting in the chair, her feet soaking in the warm water.

I smile and wave and make my way to the empty seat next to her. "For you, my dear sister." I hand her an iced coffee from Java Jitters. Sure, it's on the other side of town, but I was craving one.

"Another sacrifice." She grins.

"Right? Take notes," I say as I slip my feet into the bowl of warm water.

"So, you're thinking about staying open longer?"

"I am. Business is good, and Jasmine does a great job. She mentioned needing more hours. I thought I might try it and see if the sales make it worth it. She's already working two days a week after school. I might add some extended hours. Maybe have two late nights. That will help give her hours. She's saving for college."

"That would be nice for those who can't get off work in time to get there by five."

"That's what I was thinking too."

"Waken!" I hear two adorable little girls call out.

My head whips toward the door and the sound of their voices to find Grayson and his daughters. I smile and wave. The girls take that as their cue to come and greet me.

"Waken, what are you doing?" Harlow asks.

"I'm getting a pedicure."

"Does it tickle?" Hayden questions.

"No. It's relaxing. After my feet soak, they'll massage them and then paint my toenails."

"Oh!" Their little mouths form the perfect *O*.

"Wow. They've got this twin thing down," Lenora comments.

"Who are you?" Hayden asks.

"This is my sister, Leni. Leni, this is Harlow, and Hayden." I point to the girls. "Grayson Davis's twin daughters."

"You can tell them apart?" this comes from Grayson.

I look up at him and about swallow my tongue. Why does he have to be so damn sexy? He's wearing a pair of cargo shorts and a Mason Creek Fire T-shirt that fits as if it is tailored just for him.

"Hey, Grayson," I greet him. "Yeah, I can tell them apart."

"I thought maybe they told you when you were at the house the other day."

"It took me a while," I admit. "Your mom brings them in every week, and eventually, I figured it out.

However, if I'm not looking at both of them, I still get stumped."

The girls giggle. "That's 'cause we look idenial," Harlow states proudly.

"Identical," Grayson and I say at the same time. His eyes find mine, and the hint of a smile tilts his lips.

"Waken, guess what? You make Daddy feel wanted," Harlow says, nodding her little head.

"W-What?" I ask. I have no idea what she's talking about. I glance up at Grayson, and he's staring at me with a shocked expression on his face.

"Dat's what hims said." She looks at her sister. "Right, sissy?"

"Uh-huh. You tolded hims dat hims smelled good," Hayden adds.

"Oh, shit," Lenora mumbles under her breath, but I still hear her.

My head whips around to look at her, and the guilty expression on her face tells me everything I need to know. I did, in fact, tell Grayson Davis that he smells good, and my sister was there to witness it.

"You didn't tell me," I say through gritted teeth.

"Girls, come on. It's time for your haircuts." They scurry off to the chairs, climbing up and sitting on the booster seats without complaint. I know Grayson is still standing there, but I'm too embarrassed to look at him, so instead, I watch the girls as they chat with Anna and Faith as if they're all four best friends.

"Laken?" His voice is closer. Sucking in a deep breath, I know I have to face the music. I turn to look at him. He's closer, much closer. I open my mouth to say something, anything, but no words come out. Instead, I inhale his woodsy scent. Damn, he smells good. The next thing I know, he's bending his body close to mine, his mouth hovers over my cheek, next to my ear. "You're beautiful when you blush." His deep husky voice washes over me.

He pulls back, and my eyes find his. He must see the question because he shrugs. "Do you have plans tonight?" he asks.

"Nope. She's free," Lenora answers for me.

"Perfect. I'll be by your place around seven."

"Wait. What?"

"The girls are having a sleepover with Nana Christine and Papaw Marty, and you and I are going on a date."

"A date?"

His grin grows wider. Bending closer, he places both hands on the arms of my chair, and we're close. So close I can see the different shades of green in his eyes. "Two weeks of you being in my head. Two weeks of my daughters talking about you nonstop. Two weeks of me wondering why I can't stop thinking about you? I think it's time we find out." He stands back to his full height. "I'll be at your place at seven." He turns and walks to the front of the salon where the girls are getting haircuts. He stands between the two. His arms are crossed over his muscled chest as if he's their bodyguard.

My heart can't take the swoon, surrounded by his woodsy scent and his words. I'm a mush of feelings. My heart is racing so loud I know he can hear it, and there is an ache between my thighs.

"That, dear sister, is the definition of a panty-dropping smile."

I manage to tear my gaze from Grayson. "What are you not telling me?" I ask her. I try to glare, but I'm still reeling from Grayson in close proximity.

He can't stop thinking about me.

He wants to go on a date.

Tonight.

Holy shit!

"You might have told him that he smelled good when he put you to bed." She goes on to explain how I thought I was dreaming. And I'm mortified. "Don't do that. He's into you."

"No. He's–" I start to give a reason for his actions just minutes ago, but I've got nothing. Grayson isn't the kind of man to play games or the field. He never has been.

"Laken?" Lenora places her hand over mine that's gripping the arm of the massage chair I'm sitting in.

"Pinch me."

She throws her head back and laughs. "You're not dreaming, sister. You're going on a date with Grayson Davis."

"I have nothing to wear." My heart is racing so loudly I'm sure Grayson and his girls can hear it at the front of the salon. My palms are sweating as I think about what I have in my closet. None of it seems fitting for a date with Grayson.

"We'll go shopping when we leave here."

"It's already two thirty. We have to go to Billings, and he said seven. I'll need to shave... everything," I say, my face immediately heating as I slap my hand over my mouth.

"There's plenty of time. I'll help you get ready. Just breathe," she says soothingly.

"Leni," I whisper.

She smiles. "Just breathe, Laken. He's just a man."

"I know but, how often do you get the chance with the man of your dreams?" I take a deep breath and tell her what I'm really feeling. "It's more than that," I confess. "Those little girls... they're so sweet, and I'm already half in love with them."

Her eyes soften. "Just remember that. If this, whatever it is with Grayson, doesn't go anywhere, remember that you were half in love with them before you tried dating their daddy."

I get what she's saying. Don't let this... whatever it is, affect those two adorable little angels. Besides, it's one date, not a marriage proposal. It's dinner, and he'll see I'm the boring book nerd who's always managed to fly under his radar, and life will go back to normal. I'll go back to watching him from afar. I'll spend Thursday afternoon with his daughters just like I have the last several months, and life will be back to normal.

"Waken, wook!"

I snap out of my daze to see the twins standing in front of me. Their curls that were past their shoulders are now resting just above them.

"Wow. You ladies look beautiful." Their beaming smiles at my praise fills my heart.

"I'm hoping this makes combing through it a little easier," Grayson says, pushing his wallet back into his back pocket.

"Daddy spays stuff to make it not huwt," Harlow tells me.

"Yeah, and it smells yummy." Hayden giggles.

"Well, it sounds like Daddy is very smart."

"Oh, he is," they agree.

"Girls, why don't you go grab a sucker from the bowl? I'll be right there."

"Okay," they agree. "Bye, Waken and Waken's sister." They wave and take off for the sucker bowl that Anna is holding out for them.

Grayson steps toward me, and I'm surprised when he reaches out and tucks my hair behind my ear. "Seven, Laken. I'll see you at seven." He looks like he wants to say more, but he doesn't. He pulls his hand away and shoves it in his pocket. "Leni." He nods at my sister, then turns on his heel and walks away.

EMBRACE

I don't take my eyes off him as he offers a hand to each of the girls, and the three of them leave the salon. The door is barely shut behind them when the entire salon starts talking at once about how hot he is and how he wants me. I block them all out, feeling the crimson of my cheeks, knowing that it has to match my hair. All I can think about is my date tonight and the fact that there isn't a doubt in my mind that Tate is going to get wind of this. I can only imagine how fast her keys are going to be flying over the keyboard for her latest installment of the *MC Scoop* featuring Grayson and me.

Chapter 10

GRAYSON

A blush is a thing of beauty

Things are heating up with our fire chief and local book enthusiast.

If her blush is any indication, I'd say things are moving along quite nicely.

Is there anything more romantic than the hair tuck? I think not.

More to come from the happy couple.

Climbing into my truck, I wave through the front window at the girls. They love staying with both sets of grandparents, and although I feel guilty, like I'm pawing them off, I learned early on to take the break when I could get it. It took me a long time to accept that I didn't need to be with them all the time if I wasn't at work. I love my daughters. They are my life. However, it's good for them to get a break from me as well.

I struggled with it when we lost Holly, but the last three years have indeed shown me that it does, in fact, take a village, or in my case, a small town to raise my twin girls.

I'm barely out of the driveway when my cell rings. Seeing my dad's name flash on the dash, I reach over and hit Accept. "Hey, Dad."

"Son."

"I didn't do it." I laugh. My dad is rarely serious. He's always cutting up and finding the bright side of things in life.

"Read the *MC Scoop* lately?"

"I have."

"Well?"

"Well, what? We did, in fact, have to save a cat from a tree yesterday afternoon. The cat and all of my guys are fine. Mrs. Donaldson is happy as a lark to have her precious Pussy back. And before you ask, yes, that's the cat's name."

"No shit?" he asks with a chuckle.

"Yep."

"Good to know. However, that's not what I was asking about."

"I know." I've been meaning to talk to my parents about the *MC Scoop,* and well... the scoop of what's going on in my life, but when I pick the girls up, they're so happy to see me, I can't find it in me to send them away while I talk to my parents. And, honestly, I'm avoiding. It sounds like my time is up.

"Laken?"

"No. Yes. I mean, I don't know." I heave a heavy sigh. "She's everywhere," I tell him. "The bookstore when I meet Mom or Christine."

"She owns the bookstore, Gray," he says with laughter in his voice.

"I wasn't finished. She's at Java Jitters, the market, Pony Up. Hell, she was even at the salon today when I took the girls to get haircuts."

"She's a sweet girl. Your mother talks highly of her."

"The girls like her."

"Do you like her?"

"Yeah," I admit. "I think I do. I asked her out tonight. The girls are staying with Christine and Marty."

"How are you?"

For as much as my dad likes to joke around, he knows me better than anyone. He knows without me saying the words that tonight is hard for me. "I didn't plan on asking her out."

"Explain that," he says. I can imagine him kicked back in the recliner, one hand propped behind his head, legs crossed at the ankles.

"She's everywhere, including my thoughts. She made brownies with the girls, which I know they told you and Mom all about. Then today, we walked into the salon, and there she was. The girls ran to her, and her face lit up when she saw them. Fucking lit up, Dad. Then she called them by their names, and she was right. She can tell them apart. The girls being the girls, told her something they overheard me tell Ryder, and Laken... she blushed. It was endearing, and I just... asked her out. I have to know what this is. I have to know why I can't stop thinking about her. I don't know why she's suddenly in my life, literally around every damn corner, but I have to find out."

"I think it's just your time, son. It's time for you to pick up the pieces and let yourself be open to love again."

"I don't know how to do that. Holly, she was—" My voice cracks. "I haven't dated anyone but her since I was sixteen years old, Dad. How do I do this?"

"It's just like riding a bike, Gray. Take the girl to dinner, show her a good time. Talk, and not about the weather or the girls. Really talk to her. Find out if you have anything in common. Let yourself be open to the possibility of loving again."

"Yeah," I agree, but only half-heartedly.

"I need to get back inside. Your mom was on the phone with your aunt Darla. If I don't rescue her, she might make me sleep on the couch."

"You've never slept on the couch a day in your life."

"That's because you should never go to bed angry. You never know when your last day here on earth will be." I don't reply to that because I know all too well how short life can be. "Bring my granddaughters to visit tomorrow."

"You'll see them Monday." I laugh.

"Doesn't matter."

"I'll see you tomorrow," I tell him. He and I both know it's not to see the girls, but for him to make sure I'm okay after tonight and whatever it happens to turn out to be. Good or bad, I know that my dad and my mom will both be there. They've helped me so much since losing Holly. I hate to think about where I would have ended up or how my daughters would have ended up without their help.

I'm heading toward home but make a quick decision to turn right instead of left and head just outside the city limits of Mason Creek to the cemetery. It's been at least six months since I've been here. The last time being when I brought the girls for Holly's birthday to place flowers on her grave. It was January and blistering cold, so we didn't stay long.

Parking my truck, I make my way to Holly's grave. It's a path I've walked many times in the last three years. Most of which was the first year we lost her. When I reach my destination, I stop and take a seat on the grass, crossing my legs. My hands absently pick at the grass as I let the warm summer sun beat down on me while I collect my thoughts.

"Hey, Holls. Sorry, it's been so long since I've been by. Work is busy as ever, and the girls.... Damn, I wish you were here to see them. They both have your heart, and it shines through every damn day." I smile when I think about my late wife. In all the years we were together, and even the time before that in school, I'd never seen her be mean or cruel to anyone. She just didn't have it in her.

"They're with your parents tonight having a sleepover. They're thriving, and even though I know that's what you would want for them, my heart still aches that you're not here to see it.

"I have something to tell you." I stop there. I don't know how to tell her about Laken. I debate if I should at all, but Holly wasn't just my wife. She was my best friend. "I asked a woman out on a date tonight." I expel a heavy breath as the words pass my lips. "She's the first since I lost you. There's been no one else but you, and I'm lonely, Holls. And this woman, she's everywhere. It's like she's being thrust into my life. And the girls, they know her. They know her, and she's so good with them.

"I'm struggling with that, Holls. I'm not trying to replace you. I promise you I'm not. I just... I don't know how to do this." The heat behind my eyes begins to burn. I blink hard once, twice, three times to keep the tears at bay. "You were the love of my life."

I give myself some time to gather my composure before starting again. "You might know her, Laken Abbott. She was younger than us in school. Her older sister Lenora too. Our moms have been taking the girls to her bookstore once a week, and they adore her, Holls. And she's so good to them. She can tell them apart. You know what that means, right? She has to pay really close attention to be able to tell our daughters apart, and she can, Holly.

"She's beautiful." I whisper the words, letting the wind carry them. "It's been three years since I lost you, and she's the first woman in that time to make me want to put myself back out there. I'm sorry if this hurts you. I'm sorry if you feel as though I'm forgetting about you. I promise you I'm not. I'm just trying to move forward.

"In the last couple of weeks, it seems as though every person I know wants to dish out love advice. Would you believe that it was one of my guys at the station who really got to me? It was Canaan, and he told me I should want our daughters to see the way a man is supposed to love a woman. That it is okay for me to move on and teach them what a healthy relationship is like. For so long, I couldn't get past the fact that you were no longer here with us. I didn't want to bring a random woman into our daughters' lives. I didn't want them to feel as though I was replacing you."

I suck in a deep breath, close my eyes, and tilt my head back to the sky. "I'm lonely. I miss the intimacy and the companionship. I don't know if Laken is the one. I don't know what tonight is going to bring, but I do know she's the only other woman besides you who has affected me this way. I don't know why I just told you all of that. I guess I just... I just want you to know that I love you. That I will forever and always love you. I think that I have the room, you know? For someone else. I think I'm ready."

Climbing to my feet, I kiss the tips of my fingers and place them against her headstone. "I'll bring the girls by to see you real soon." With that, I turn and make my way to my truck. There are so many emotions swirling through me. I'm not sure which one I should address first.

I'm sad. This isn't how we had our life planned. She was supposed to be here with me, helping me raise our daughters. Holly should be here watching them grow up. The tragic loss of her in our lives will forever leave a hole where she should have been.

I'm nervous. Holly and I started dating when I was sixteen years old. She was my everything, and now she's not here. I have no doubt that if she still walked this earth that she would still be mine.

I'm excited though. Laken is gorgeous with her long red hair and those big hazel eyes. And she has a crush on me. I can't help the smile that tilts my lips. She thinks I smell good, and I know for certain she does as well.

I'm turned on. Just thinking about the blush on her cheeks drives me mad. She's all I've been able to think about. Earlier today, at the salon, I got too close. Her scent, something fruity, wrapped around me, the same as the night I carried her to her apartment. I want to kiss her lips. I need to know if they're as soft as they look. And her skin, I'm sure, will be like silk under my touch.

I don't know what tonight is going to hold, but I know that I have to try. Laken makes me want to try, and that's something. That's me feeling again. More than just love for my daughters and pain from the loss of my late wife.

She makes me want to live.

Chapter 11

LAKEN

"THIS IS A BAD IDEA," I tell my sister. I'm sitting on a kitchen chair while she does my makeup.

"Explain that statement," she says, as she continues to brush eyeshadow across my eyelids.

I don't reply. I can't explain it. It's not a bad idea, not really. It's just that I'm nervous as hell. I've crushed on Grayson for years. *Years*. For some reason, we've been thrust into each other's lives a lot lately, and well, now we're going on a date.

"You do realize you are the first woman he's asked out since losing his wife."

"How do you know that?"

"Really, Laken? This is Mason Creek. Besides, the *MC Scoop* says so, so you know it must be true." She chuckles. "Furthermore, you live here. Have you seen or heard of him dating? You know damn good and well if he had, Tate would have been all over that."

"No. He's— No, not that I know of." She's right. There's nothing that happens in Mason Creek without everyone in town finding out about it. Part of the reason is Tate and her blog, and the other half, well, that's just small-town living. It's a blessing and a curse. Everyone knows everyone's business, but at the same time, we rally around our own.

We're more than just neighbors. We're family.

"Breathe, Laken. You're going to dinner with a man who is clearly interested in you. We both know that Grayson isn't one to play around. He's one of the good ones. It's just dinner."

"Right." I nod. "Just dinner."

"Exactly." She pulls back and smiles. "You look beautiful, little sis."

Standing, I make my way to the small bathroom and stare at my reflection in the mirror. My long red hair hangs down my back in its natural beach wave. I'm wearing an emerald green sundress and strappy sandals. My makeup is light, and the green she used on my eyes makes the hazel color pop. Then again, it could be the color of the dress, and maybe it's the combination of the two.

"Am I overdressed?" I ask Lenora.

"No. He said dinner, and your outfit is the best mix if it's fancy or casual. This works." She waves her hands at me.

"Thank you for helping me." I go to her, wrapping my arms around her in a hug. "I'm so glad you're home. I've missed you."

"I missed you too." She steps out of my embrace. "I'm going to get out of here, so he doesn't think you need your big sister to hold your hand."

"I do, though."

She smiles. "You don't need me, Laken. You're beautiful, and he's going to swallow his tongue when he sees you." She winks. "Just be you. Be real. Don't hide who you are, and don't pretend to be someone you think he would want. If he doesn't see the real you and fall in love with you, then he doesn't deserve you."

"Hold up. No one said anything about falling in love."

She shrugs. "Be you because you are incredible. And he sees that, or tonight wouldn't be happening."

"I love you."

"Love you too. Have fun, and call me after."

"I will." With another hug, she's out the door, and I'm alone.

Glancing at the clock on the stove, I see it's fifteen minutes before seven. He could be here at any minute. Grabbing my small purse, making sure I have what I need, my phone, keys, and wallet, I lock up my apartment and head down the stairs. I wait at the back door. Then I realize I don't know if he's coming to the front or the back, and I don't have his number to ask him or guide him in any way. I pace back and forth, wondering if I should just go stand out in front of the building. Chances are he would see me before pulling around back. I'm digging for my keys to unlock the door that separates the small entryway and my bookstore when there's a knock on the back door. My pulse quickens. I stop pacing and take in a couple of deep breaths before making my way to the door.

Pulling the door open, I can't help but smile when I see Grayson standing there. He's wearing a pair of dark jeans that look as though they were made just for him and a black fitted T-shirt. "Hi," I say lamely.

"Laken," he breathes. He steps toward me and presses his lips to my cheek. "You're beautiful." His words, along with his hot breath, fan across my cheek, causing a shiver to race down my spine.

"Thank you. You look handsome." His words and his reaction give me the courage I need to speak what's on my mind. Lenora's right. I need to be me. "I wasn't sure where we were going, so I didn't really know what to wear."

"This—" His hand trails down my arm, leaving goose bumps in its wake until his hand is clasped with mine. "—is perfect. I thought we could drive over to Billings to that new steakhouse."

"Sounds great." I turn and pull the door closed, checking to make sure it's locked.

"I'm not trying to hide this," he says as he drops my hand only to place his on the small of my back as he leads me to his truck. "I'm sure Tate is going to hear about it regardless. I've just been craving steak. I also thought we might get a night of not feeling as though we're in a fishbowl with all of Mason Creek watching us."

"Billings is perfect," I assure him. "And are you sure you want to do this? You know you're right about Tate. She's going to get wind of this, and the entire town is going to know."

"Do you want to hide this?" He points his index finger at his chest, then back at me.

"No."

"Then I'm sure." He gives me a charming smile as he grabs for the door of his truck to open it for me.

"Thank you." I reach in, grab the handle, and hoist myself inside. I'm quick to drop in the seat, hoping I didn't just give him a show with this dress and his tall-ass truck.

"Buckle up," he says before closing the door and jogging around to the driver's side, and sliding behind the wheel.

"How was the rest of your day?" I ask.

"Good. I took the girls to Christine and Marty. They're having a sleepover. They do the same with my parents one weekend a month. It's become something the girls really look forward to."

"I'm sure it's nice to have a break. Please don't take that the wrong way." I rush to get the words out. "Those girls of yours are something special. I just mean it has to be hard on you keeping it all together on your own." Damnit, I'm messing this up. "I'm sorry. I didn't mean—" I start but stop midsentence when Grayson reaches over the console and places his hand over mine.

"It's nice to get a break. I love my daughters. They're my life, but you're right. Being a single parent is hard, and the break is very much appreciated." He pauses. "It took me a while after losing Holly to realize I didn't need to be with them all the time. That it was okay to get a break now and then. That doesn't mean I love them any less."

"Of course not. That's not what I meant at all."

"I know that." He gives my hand a gentle squeeze. "I just mean, it took me some time to get that through my thick skull."

"I'm happy to help anytime. You know, if you need a sitter or something. We can make brownies or cookies or something."

He glances over, a small smile playing on his lips before darting his eyes right back to the road. "Thank you, Laken."

The way he says my name, all deep and... sexual. Okay, so it's not sexual, but it turns me on all the same, which has me shifting in my seat. I'd be happy to sit here next to him, just letting him say my name over and over again. Hell, he could read me his grocery list, and I'd be happy to sit and listen.

The remainder of the drive is small talk, but not awkward small talk. I settle back into my seat and enjoy the feel of his hand over mine as we talk about our favorite music, food, and an array of other topics as we get to know one another.

"Wow, this place is packed," I say as we pull into the parking lot of the steakhouse.

"Do you want to go somewhere else?"

"No. I mean, if you do, that's fine."

"Let's see how long the wait is. Stay put." He points at me before pulling the keys from the ignition and climbing out of the truck. My gaze follows him as he walks to my door, tugging it open. He offers me his hand, and I take it willingly.

With his hand on the small of my back, we make our way inside. He leads us to the hostess, and she tells us the wait is only about ten minutes, so we decide to stay.

"Laken?"

Turning to look over my shoulder, I see Grady and Charlotte. "Hey." I smile and wave.

"Fancy seeing you here," she says with a smirk.

"Gray." Grady nods at Grayson.

"Looks like we all had the same idea." Grayson laughs.

I want to look over at him to see if he's nervous that we ran into his friend and mine or if he's as calm as his voice makes him out to be. He doesn't remove his hand from the small of my back, and I'm taking that as a good sign.

"This is new," Charlotte says, pointing between us.

"First date," Grayson explains.

"Interesting," Charlotte muses.

"Jackson, party of two," the hostess calls out.

"You want to join us?" Grady offers.

"Nah, maybe next time," Grayson answers.

"Thanks, though." I wave at them. I wait until they walk away with the hostess to turn and look at Grayson. "That didn't take long." I smile.

He leans in close, his lips next to my ear. "Knew it would happen. I have nothing to hide, Laken."

I nod and turn back around. His close proximity has rendered me speechless, and even if I could form words, what would I say? You haven't dated since losing your wife over three years ago, so I thought you would want to ease into this? It's not my place. Only Grayson knows how he feels and if he's ready to date. From his actions and the fact we're standing here because he asked me to dinner, I'd say he's ready.

Or at least he's getting there.

"Davis, party of two."

"That's us," Grayson speaks up.

"If you'll follow me," the hostess says politely.

With his hand still on the small of my back, we follow behind our hostess, who seats us at a back booth, hidden away in the corner of the restaurant. "Thank you," I tell her as I slide into the booth, as Grayson slides into the other. I expected to be nervous, but I'm surprisingly not. I'm comfortable with Grayson. I don't care who else is here that we might know. I don't care if we happen to run into a few familiar faces. All I care about is that right now, I have his full attention and he has mine.

Chapter 12

GRAYSON

OUR MEAL HAS LONG SINCE been finished, and we've both declined dessert, yet here we sit in this back corner booth of the restaurant, neither of us ready to leave. Tonight has been... incredible. Laken is not only drop-dead gorgeous, but she's also easy to talk to, kind, smart, funny, and she's just... a breath of fresh air for me. For all of my nerves tonight, she eased every one of them. As we sit here talking about anything and everything, it's as if we've been close friends for years.

"I guess we should go," she says, looking around the restaurant. "They probably want to clean up and go home."

"If we must," I sigh dramatically, making her laugh. Sliding out of the booth, I offer her my hand, and she takes it without hesitation. The parking lot is pretty empty as we make our way to my truck. I open the door for her, and she climbs inside. Her hair falls over her eyes, and I reach out to tuck it behind her ear, just as I did earlier today. "Laken—" I start but have to stop to swallow hard. This is a big deal for me. "Tonight, thank you for making this so easy. You're incredible, and if I forget to tell you later, it's been a long damn time since I've felt this... relaxed. That's all thanks to you." Before even I realize what I'm doing, I lean in and press a kiss on her cheek. "Buckle up," I whisper before pulling back and closing her door.

I take my time walking around the front of my truck. Why? Because I want to kiss her. Before I lost my wife, it was only ever her from the time I was sixteen years old. And now... Laken. I can't explain this pull I feel toward her, but I'll be damned if I don't want to explore it. Explore her.

The drive home is much more relaxed than the drive to Billings. Not that it was awkward; we're just more comfortable with one another after a night of talking about anything and everything. Reaching over the console, I lace her fingers with mine. "Earlier today, I went to the cemetery." I don't know why I say it, but it feels good to get that confession out in the open. It's not like I'm cheating. Hell, this is our first date, but I don't know. I guess I just need her to know.

Her hand squeezes mine. "I can't imagine how hard this is for you."

I want to pull the truck over and kiss the hell out of her. So many women in the past three years have tried to hit on me. They all promise the same thing, let me help you forget about her. That's what they don't understand. I never want to forget about Holly. She was my first love. She gave me two little girls who are my world. I never want to forget her, and the understanding in Laken's words would bring me to my knees if I weren't already sitting.

"Are you in a hurry to get home?" I ask instead.

"I'm all yours for as long as you want me." Her words are softly spoken, and I can't help but wonder if they have a double meaning.

Instead of taking the road that will lead us back to Mason Creek, I turn off to a mountain lookout. I found it one weekend when Ryder and I were hiking. I just want to talk to her some more. I know that the prying eyes of Mason Creek will be all over this date, but I want some more time with her.

"Where are we?" She leans forward in her seat to look out the front window.

"It's a lookout Ryder and I found on one of our hikes. The view is great during the day. I've never been up here at night." I park the truck, roll down the windows, and turn off the engine. Removing my seat belt, I turn in my seat to face her.

She does the same. Her smile is lit up by the light of the moon filtering in through the truck windows. "The stars are brighter up here."

I don't bother looking, not when the view right beside me is better than any star in the sky. "I wanted to tell her about our date." I carry on with my previous confession. "I know that makes me sound crazy, but it felt like something I needed to do."

"Not crazy at all. Everyone heals differently. There's no timeline or handbook for these kinds of things. We all have to do whatever it is that gets us through the day."

"Not everyone feels that way."

"How they feel doesn't matter, Grayson. You and those two little girls are all that matters in this situation. You have to do what you feel is right."

I squeeze her hand. "This feels right, Laken. I never thought I would be ready to date. I was convinced my daughters were enough, and they are but this—" I lift our joined hands to my lips. "This feels good too."

"I'm not going to pretend I know what you went through or how you feel. What I can tell you is I will always be open and honest with you. So, here's my honesty. Tonight has been the best date I've ever been on. I enjoy your company, and if you're willing, I'd love to do it again. With that being said, I'm not rushing you. You take your time and tell me when you're ready. All I ask is that you tell me when this isn't what you want any longer. No harm, no foul. I just don't want to be the girl sitting around waiting for your attention when you no longer want to give it to me."

"Is that what you want, Laken? You want my attention." My voice is husky even to my own ears.

"Yes. I also don't want to take your attention away from your daughters. I know that those little girls come first, and I'm okay with that. However, if there is a weekend you have free and you want to have dinner, I'd like to be considered on the list of people you would call to keep you company."

"I really want my arms around you right now."

"Yeah?" she asks, equal parts surprised and interested if I'm reading her tone right.

"Damn console," I say, making her laugh.

"I think we can fix that." She turns to face the front window and bends at the waist. A minute later, she lifts her sandals in the air and then tosses them back to the floorboard. She takes it a step further and climbs up on her knees in the seat.

I get the hint at what she's going to do, and I reach beside me and push the button that makes my seat slide back as far as it will go. I'm a tall guy, so it doesn't give us much more space, but that doesn't seem to stop Laken. She climbs, turns with her back to me, and scoots her ass up on the console, and the need to have her in my arms is too strong to wait a second longer. With my hands on her hips, I slide her the rest of the way back until she's sitting on my lap, her legs propped up on the console.

"That's better." She smiles up at me.

I wrap my arms around her in an embrace, holding her close to my chest. I close my eyes and breathe her in. I wait for the panic to hit me that this woman isn't my wife, but it never comes. There's a ping of sadness in my heart, but there's also love for

Holly that will forever be there. No matter what my future holds, there's a piece of my heart that will forever be hers.

Laken snuggles up to me, resting her head on my shoulder, and lets me hold her. I don't know how, but it's as if she knows I need this connection. I need intimacy from her, even if it is just an embrace.

"Holly was my first real date. I'd just turned sixteen. I'd been on group things or had my parents take us places, but she was the first woman I ever knocked on her door and escorted her to my truck for a proper date. She was my first, and now there's you."

She lifts her head and looks at me. "You don't have to tell me any of this."

"I know, and that's why I want to. You're different. I wish I could tell you the number of times I've been hit on since losing Holly. They all wanted to make me forget." I pause, letting her ponder my words. "I don't want to forget, Laken. I also want to live. I want to move forward. I want to love again."

"Tonight is a good first step," she says, snuggling back into my chest.

We spend the next two hours talking, our conversation flowing freely just as it did at the restaurant. All the while, I hold her in my arms. I don't take it further, and she seems to be content to give me whatever it is that I need from her. When she yawns, I know I have to take her home.

"You ready to head home?"

"If you are," she replies, her voice groggy.

Unable to stop myself, I place a kiss on the top of her head. "Get buckled in, and we'll head home." She moves back to the passenger seat and bends over to slide her feet back into her sandals before pulling her seat belt over her chest and smiling at me. "Ready."

I want to kiss her.

I don't know if that's a thing, kissing on the first date. I'm new at this, and the last time I had a first date, I was a horny teenager. Funnily, I don't feel far off from that now. I guess I should have called Ryder or one of the guys and asked them the protocol. No, that's not how I roll. I'm going to do what feels right. Open and honest. That's Laken and that's me. That's who we are.

I hold her hand in mine all the way back to Mason Creek. When I pull up behind her building, I shut off the engine. "Stay there," I tell her, grabbing my keys and climbing out of the truck. I rush to her door.

"You know, you don't have to open doors for me."

"You know, if my momma found out I didn't, she'd kick my ass. And you know damn good and well there are eyes everywhere in this town." I give her a charming smile, one she playfully rolls those big hazel eyes to.

With my hand on the small of her back, I lead her to the back entrance of her building. The one that I know she owns from a small inheritance left to her from her grandmother. When she opens the door, she holds it open, allowing me to step inside. It's a small open foyer area. There's a staircase that leads up to her apartment, and another door that I assume leads into her bookstore.

"Thank you for tonight. It was a lot of fun." She smiles up at me.

My palm rests against her cheek, and the need to kiss her grows stronger. "Can I kiss you?"

Her answer is to grip my shirt, stand on her tiptoes, and press her soft lips against mine. She falls back to her feet way too soon for my liking, but that's okay. This is only our first date. Sliding my arm around her waist, I hold her tight against my chest. I could stand here and hold her all night, but I know she's tired, so I pull back.

"When can we do this again?" I ask. I'm not playing games and waiting however many days some stupid dating protocol calls for. I've heard the guys talk about it over the years, and that's not me.

"When you have the free time, call me."

"About that. I'm going to need your number."

She smiles and holds out her hand. I dig my phone out of my back pocket and swipe at the screen, unlocking it before handing it to her. "I have to keep it locked, or the girls will sneak and watch videos every chance they get."

"I can see them doing that." She chuckles, handing my phone back to me.

"Thank you, Laken. I enjoyed your company." I relish holding her in my arms and the feel of her lips pressed to mine.

"It was the best first date."

"Definitely. Lock up after me." I lean in and kiss the corner of her mouth. "Night, Laken."

"Night, Grayson. Drive safe."

"Always." I step outside and wait until I hear the lock slide into place before walking back to my truck. The entire drive home, I let the night play on repeat.

The fear, the nerves, the guilt, it's all disappeared. One night with the gorgeous redhead, and she's managed to ease them all.

Chapter 13

LAKEN

M Y ALARM BLARES IN MY ear at fifteen minutes before seven. I don't open the store until eight, but I'm still exhausted. I stayed up way too late talking to Grayson on the phone once the girls went to bed. This has become our nightly ritual over the last two weeks. This coming weekend the girls are staying with their grandparents, so that means it's date night, and I'm excited to get to spend some time with him one-on-one.

I feel a little guilty being excited that the girls are going to stay with their grandparents. It's not that I don't want them with us, but Grayson isn't ready to tell them about us, and I understand that. So we haven't been on another date since our first. Well, we have, if you count me stopping by to bake cookies with the girls and stealing kisses with Grayson.

I also go over a couple of nights a week after the girls are in bed. Thankfully, it's summer, so we cuddle out on the back deck underneath the stars. I feel as if we're teenagers sneaking around, but I understand why we're doing it. His daughters need to come first, and I not only understand that, but I respect it.

Grabbing my phone, I'm already smiling before I even see his message. That's become a new routine for us as well. Good morning and goodnight texts. They're the highlight of my day. What am I saying? Any messages, or calls, or visits from Grayson are the highlight of my day.

Today, he's coming to the store to eat lunch with me. We're not hiding from the town, just his daughters. I asked him what he would do if someone mentioned us in front of the girls. He said he didn't think anyone in Mason Creek would do that, and I happen to agree. They might be nosey as hell and be all up in everyone's business, but they wouldn't involve the girls in that gossip. Everyone in our small town knows they lost their mother tragically, and they also know that I'm the first woman Grayson has dated since his wife. They'll tread carefully as they talk about us.

Gotta love small-town living.

Grayson's message is a picture of him lying in bed. The spot next to him is empty.

Grayson: Wish you were here.

I smile and take a similar photo to send back to him.

Me: I have a spot for you too.

That's one of the things that I love about our relationship. We've spent a lot of time talking and getting to know one another, and there is an honesty and a trust between us that I've never had with any other man.

Grayson: *I like the sound of that.*

Grayson: *Are we still on for lunch today?*

Me: *Yep.*

Grayson: *Noon?*

Me: *I'm flexible.*

Grayson: *As long as we don't get a run around then, I'll be there.*

Me: *Be safe.*

Tossing my phone on the bed, I throw off the covers and get moving. I need to shower and put the Crock-Pot on low. I made beef and noodles yesterday, and I figure we can eat that with lunch and the homemade biscuits I made last night while Grayson and I were on the phone. I know he'll have to get back to the station, and I didn't want to spend half of our lunch together with him having to go and grab something for us. That happened last week. This week, I'm being selfish.

I want all of his time that he has to offer me.

At precisely noon on the dot, the chime on the door alerts me to a customer. Glancing toward the door, I smile when I see Grayson. My smile grows even wider when I remember that my last customer just left, and we have the place to ourselves, at least until the next customer arrives. I don't know how long that will be, so I rush out from behind the counter and meet him halfway. A quick peck to his lips is all he gets before I'm taking him by the hand and dragging him with me to the foyer that leads to my place. I can hear the door and even see it from this angle, but they won't be able to see us.

"Laken—" he starts, but I cut him off when I push him up against the wall and pull his lips to mine. The kiss is wild and unhinged, exactly the way I feel when I'm with him.

I groan when Grayson slows the kiss, resting his forehead to mine. "That's a welcome I could get used to."

"I missed you."

"I missed you too."

"Go on upstairs and make yourself a plate. The Crock-Pot is on the counter, and there are biscuits in a container on the counter next to it."

"Are you going to eat too?"

"Yes. I'm right behind you. I'll need to make a plate and then come right back down."

"I'll make you one. Go on back out to the register."

"Are you sure?" My heart pitter-patters in my chest. It's something simple, him making me a plate, but he's one of the good ones. One of the men who will make sure your needs are met.

"Yes." He kisses me quickly. "I'm sure."

"Thank you."

"You can pay me with more of those kisses." He winks and, taking the stairs two at a time, heads up to my place.

Surprisingly, no customers arrive by the time he comes back downstairs with a bowl for each of us. We move to sit in the little office behind the register so we can eat.

"How is your day so far?" I ask him.

"Quiet, which in my line of work is a good thing." He takes a huge bite of stew and groans. "This is so good," he says, diving in for another bite.

"Thank you."

"How about you? Been busy today?" he asks.

"Not really. Thankfully, the patrons of Mason Creek are giving us time together today."

"Oh, they know I'm here. It wouldn't surprise me if they were timing my visit." He laughs.

"You're probably right," I agree.

"How were the girls this morning?"

"They were in an excellent mood when I agreed to let them call you and see if you wanted to bake with them tonight." He grins.

"Aw, that's a good plan you came up with last night. I love spending time with them."

"They love it too. Although I confess, my idea was purely selfish. I wanted to see you."

"Well, I happen to approve regardless of the reason." I smile at him.

"I'm going to tell them," he assures me.

"It's fine, Grayson. I understand the position you're in. Your daughters come first."

"I just want to ease them into this. Not only that, but I don't want them to get their hearts broken."

"I'd break my own first." I mean that with all that I am. I would never hurt those girls or Grayson.

"You're amazing, you know that?" he asks, leaning over the small space between our chairs and kissing me softly.

"You and your daughters make it easy." I want to tell him that I won't hurt them because the three of them already own my heart, but it's too soon for that. I bite back the words as the chime rings on the front door.

"Duty calls." I stand, placing my half-empty bowl on the desk.

"Laken?" Grayson calls. I turn to find him standing right behind me. His hand slides behind my neck as his lips descend on mine. He kisses me, taking his sweet time, but I'm not complaining. "Thank you for lunch. I'm going to head back to the station. I'll see you tonight?"

"Yes. I'm going to run to the store to get what we need as soon as I close, and I'll be over."

"Tell me what you need, and I'll get it."

"I got it. You get the girls and get dinner started."

"Bossy."

"Organized. Dinner and baking off the to-do list, and we get more time together. The four of us," I add.

"My girl is smart." He kisses me again, making me forget anything and everything but him.

"Laken, are you hiding back— Oh, now I see why you ignored the chime of the bell." Justine laughs. "I'll just be out here."

"I was just leaving," Grayson says, keeping his eyes on me. "I'll see you later."

"Definitely," I agree.

Another quick kiss, and he steps away. "Justine, tell Tucker I said hello," Grayson says as he steps past her and heads for the door.

"Damn," Justine says, fanning her face with her hands. "That was hot."

"It was just a kiss."

"Just a kiss, my ass. Your face is flushed, and you're holding onto the door frame for support. That man literally kissed your knees weak."

"He's really good at it," I tell her, and she throws her head back in laughter.

"Looks like it. I love my man," she says, placing her hands on her baby bump. "I'm already pregnant, but if I weren't, that kiss I walked in on would have done the trick," she jokes.

"Stop."

"Hot, Laken. So hot."

"What are you doing here?" I ask, changing the subject. I don't need her to tell me how hot it was. I lived it. I still feel the heat of his lips pressed against mine.

"Is that any way to talk to your best friend?" She mock glares at me.

"I'm sorry."

She waves me off. "Don't be. You're kiss drunk." I don't correct her. "Anyway, I've already read all the pregnancy books you sold me. I need more."

I smile at her. "I thought you might. I ordered a few more just for you." I reach under the register for the books that I ordered and put them back just for her.

"How much do I owe you?" she asks, pulling out her wallet.

"Nothing. These are on me. It's an early baby gift."

"You don't have to do that."

"I know, but I want to."

"Bring it in, bestie." She holds her arms open, and I walk into them, hugging her as tight as the baby will allow.

"Let me know if you need more after these," I tell her.

"When this little one thinks it's time to play soccer in the middle of the night, these will keep me company."

"Oh, I read a good romance—" I start, but she cuts me off.

"Pregnancy hormones are legit, and I can't be reading that in the middle of the night. Poor Tucker would never get rested." She grins.

"Fair enough."

"I should get going. We need to have dinner, the four of us. Soon."

"I'll see what I can do."

With another hug, she leaves just in time for me to hear my phone alert me to a message.

> **Grayson:** I miss you already.
>
> **Me:** You know how to make a girl smile.
>
> **Grayson:** You're the only woman I want to make smile. As for the girls, that's reserved for my daughters.
>
> **Me:** I miss you too.
>
> **Grayson:** I'll see you soon.
>
> **Me:** Yes, you will.

Placing my phone on my desk, I grab my now cold half-eaten bowl of stew and scarf it down. Grabbing Grayson's, I run them upstairs, dropping them in the sink and rushing back downstairs to get back to work.

Chapter 19

GRAYSON

I T'S FINALLY SATURDAY, AND TONIGHT is date night with Laken. I can't tell you how much I've looked forward to this night. I haven't seen her since Wednesday night when she came over for dinner and baked with the girls. That's becoming something that all four of us look forward to. We still haven't told the girls that we're dating, and with each passing day, it gets harder and harder to conceal my feelings for her. I want to tell them soon. They love her, and she's so damn good with them.

She stayed long after they went to bed on Wednesday night. The memory of making out like teenagers on the couch makes my heart splutter in my chest. I'm in deep with her. I used to think I'd never find love again, but that's before Laken Abbott. I still feel some level of guilt. I just keep reminding myself that Holly is gone, and I have to keep living. For me. For my girls and for Holly.

Aside from date night, I still have stuff I have to get done today. I have to push Laken out of my mind so I can get them done. First up, getting the girls dressed and their hair at least combed, and off to the grocery store we go.

"Girls!" I call out for them. The slapping of their little feet against the hardwood floor tells me they're on their way. They appear in front of me wearing wide smiles, and— "Is that makeup?"

"Uh-huh. It's pwetty, right, Daddy?" Hayden asks.

"Where did you get makeup?"

"Nana." Harlow shrugs. Shrugs! Like a damn teenager. Lord help me. When they reach their teen years, I'm going to need it.

"Which one?" I'm going to need them to be more specific so I don't go off on the wrong nana.

"Nana Jackie," they answer together.

"Perfect," I say sarcastically, not that my daughters pick up on it. "Let's get you cleaned up. We need to go to the store."

"Okay." They take off running down the hall, with me hot on their tail. Following them into the bathroom to help them wash up, I freeze when I see the mess before me. There is makeup everywhere. As in all over the counter, the mirror, and the walls.

"Girls, you know makeup goes on your face only, right?"

"We know," they tell me.

"Of course you do," I mutter.

"All right, strip down. Time for another bath."

"We just did our makeup."

"I know, but it's illegal for little girls to go out in public with this much makeup on, and it's all over everything. So you both need another bath."

"But—" they start, and I glare at them, crossing my arms over my chest. I've perfected the dad look over the years, and they know when they get "the look" that I mean business.

They start stripping while I get the water running. My cell rings in my pocket, and I think about ignoring it, but it might be Laken. Fishing it out of my back pocket, I see my mother's calling. "Are your ears ringing?" I ask, instead of saying hello.

"They're not. Should they be?" she asks, curious.

"You gave them makeup." My tone is accusing, and that's okay because the girls sold her out, so we know she's guilty.

"I did. They promised me they wouldn't use it unsupervised."

"Mom," I groan. "They're four."

"But they are very smart for four."

"You can't give them makeup and not tell me about it. I need to keep it hidden, just like the Play-Doh.

There are times for that kind of playtime. This morning when I have errands to run is not that time.”

She laughs. Laughs! “Calm down, Gray, it’s just a little makeup.”

“Tell that to my daughters who are covered in the shit and my poor bathroom.”

“Daddy, dats a bad word,” Hayden points out.

“Daddy slipped. I’m sorry,” I tell her.

“Dats okay.” Harlow forgives me for both of them.

“How about I come over and help?”

“You don’t have to. You’ve got sh—stuff to do as well.” I’m on edge because I have to go to the bank, the post office, and the grocery store. And I’m missing Laken something fierce.

“It’s fine. I was actually calling to tell you that you could drop them off earlier than planned. Your dad and I are headed to Billings, and we wanted to take the girls with us. I promised them a new outfit.”

“You spoil them,” I state the obvious.

“You’re damn right we do,” my dad chimes in.

“Hi, Dad. I didn’t know you were listening.”

“We’re already in the truck, son. We’ll see you in a few.”

I swallow my pride. “Thank you.”

“See you soon,” Mom says.

“Well, Nana and Pap are on their way over. So we better get this bath out of the way. Then, the two of you are going to give me all of your makeup.”

"Don't frow it away, Daddy," Hayden pleads.

"We wove it," Harlow adds.

"I'm not going to throw it away. However, if you get into it again without permission and supervision, it will be in the trash. Got it?"

"Got it," they reply.

A half an hour later, I'm in my truck and heading to town. My parents have the girls at my place. They found the makeup all over the bathroom amusing. I didn't bother to remind them that if I had pulled a stunt like that when I was younger, I'd be grounded for life. It's no use, not when it comes to my girls. They spoil them rotten. Normally, I'm okay with it, but makeup? Really? They're four. I can't believe Mom really thought that they wouldn't use it unless supervised. She's delusional.

Sighing, I make my way into the city limits of Mason Creek. My first stop is the post office. I need to mail a few bills that I can't pay online, and I'm out of stamps. I keep my head down and don't make eye contact with anyone. I don't have time to chat. I need to get to the bank before it closes as well.

The drive-through is packed, so I opt to head inside. They won't refuse to help me if I'm in the building. Yes, I know this from personal experience. The cool air conditioning hits me as I stand in line behind Tucker.

"Hey, man," I greet him.

"What's up, Gray?" he asks.

"Errands, you?"

"The same. One more after this. Gotta get my girl some ice cream."

I nod. "I remember those days." When Holly was pregnant with the girls, I was always making trips for anything and everything she might have had a craving for. That's the least I could do.

"I saw your girl earlier," he says nonchalantly.

"Oh, yeah?" I hope I sound casual. That's what I'm going for. I don't want to show him the jealousy that stirs in my gut. I don't know if I've ever felt this level of jealousy before.

He's just making casual conversation. He doesn't know I haven't laid eyes on her since Wednesday. He doesn't know I'm going crazy not seeing her or that tonight is date night. He doesn't know I'm tempted to lock her away in my house and ravish her. I might want to do that, but I won't. It's bad enough we're hiding us from the girls. I don't want her in any way to think that she's some dirty little secret.

He nods. "I stopped at One More Chapter and picked up a couple of books I asked Laken to order for me. Justine is reading all these mommy pregnancy books, and I feel like she's learning things I need to brush up on my knowledge, so I asked Laken to order me some dad books," he says, running his fingers through his hair.

"You'll be fine, Tuck," I tell him. "Trust me. If I can raise two on my own, you and Justine are going to kickass as a team of two for one baby. Besides, you already have a great teenager, you obviously know what you're doing."

"Thanks, man. I'm nervous, but damn, I can't wait. I wasn't sure I would ever have more kids. Hell, I wasn't sure I'd ever let myself fall again, but here we are."

I nod in understanding. I know all too well what it feels like to have something you never thought you would. In my case, I never thought that I would have it again. Tucker steps forward to the window, and I follow him to the next available teller.

An hour later, everything on my list is marked off. I'm back in the truck headed home when Dad calls. "Hey, I'm almost back home."

"We wanted to see if we could go ahead and leave with the girls?"

"Yeah, that's fine. Tell them I love them and to be good."

"They're angels," he responds.

"Sure they are." I chuckle. "Be safe."

"We will. You do the same."

"Thanks, Dad." He doesn't mention that I'm going out with Laken tonight, but he knows that I am. I'm grateful he didn't mention it in front of the twins. They would have insisted that they go. I love my daughters. I do. I love them with every inch of my soul, but I need Laken. I need some time with her, and tonight is finally our chance.

An idea pops into my head. Dialing her number, I wait for her to answer as I guide my truck to park behind her building.

"Hey, I was just thinking about you."

"You're all I think about," I counter.

"Grayson." The way she breathes my name has my cock twitching in my shorts.

"Can you meet me at the back door?"

"Sure. Wait. My back door?"

"That's the one."

"Are you here?"

"Come down and find out." She squeals and tells me she'll be right down. Not a minute later, the back door to her building is flying open, and she's launching herself at me. Her legs wrap around my waist, and her arms wrap around my neck.

"I don't know why you're here, but I'll take it," she says, burying her face in my neck.

"I'm on my way home from the store, and I wanted to see you."

"I missed you too, Gray," she says, kissing me loudly on the lips. "Wait." She pulls back to look at me. "Where are the girls?" She tries to move out of my arms, and I grip her ass a little tighter, holding her to me.

"Mom and Dad wanted to take them to Billings with them. They just left."

"So we can start date night now?" she asks.

"Well, yes, but I have a back seat full of groceries."

"I'll follow you home."

"Pack a bag first."

She nods. "Already done." She kisses me one more time and loosens her legs, and I let her.

"Drive safe. I'll see you soon."

"I'm right behind you." She smiles up at me, and my heart does that thing it does whenever she's near. It's like it skips a beat, squeezes, and flips over all at the same time.

"How about I follow you?" I ask her.

She grins. "Fine, you twisted my arm. Let me grab my stuff." She darts back inside, and I head back to my truck. Her excitement is infectious and a relief. I'm glad she's just as excited about our time together as I am. Not that I needed validation, but that makes this—me falling for her—so much easier. She's in this just as deep as I am. We need to tell the girls soon. I don't know how much longer I can pretend she's not someone special to me in front of them.

Scrolling through my phone while I wait, I get a notification for a new post from the *MC Scoop*. I hate that I follow Tate's blog, but Laken and I have been a hot topic, so it's something I feel like I need to watch.

The latest from the *MC Scoop*.

A tryst, you say?

I think so!

It appears that our fire chief and resident bookstore owner are indulging in a little alone time. Rumor has it they shared quite the greeting earlier today. Things are definitely heating up between the two.

Stay tuned for more Grayken!

"Dinner was delicious," Laken says, pushing away from the table.

"I know my way around the grill," I boast, making her laugh.

"So modest," she teases.

"Hey, when you've got it, you've got it."

"Stop." She's laughing as she tosses the dishtowel at me.

"How about we take a drive?" I want nothing more than to take her up to my room to ravish her, but that's not what I want her to think this is. She's not some hidden booty call when I don't have my daughters. As long as I'm spending time with her, the rest will come. Besides, she's staying with me tonight. I know that I'm going to bed with her snuggled in my arms. However, it's just after eight, and even though I'd love nothing more, it's too early to go to bed just yet.

"Sure. Let me grab my shoes." She disappears into the living room to grab her shoes, and we're out the door. "Where are we going?" she asks.

"I don't really have a destination. I just felt like driving some backroads with my girl."

"Gotta love living in a small town."

"Do you? Love your life in Mason Creek?"

She nods. "I do. Sure, I hate that Tate is all up in everyone's business. I hate that Hattie and Hazel not only gossip but meddle, but I also love this town because of it. They might meddle or gossip, but I know that if I needed any of them, they would be the first in line and the first to rally the troops."

"I agree with you. It's nice raising the girls here. Not just because it's where I grew up, but because we know everyone, and they know us. It's safe, and you're right. The meddling and the gossip are done out of love."

"You're taking me to your work?" she asks when we pull up behind the fire station.

"Not exactly. Stay there." I point my finger at her telling her I'm serious. Grabbing my phone and keys, I rush around the truck and open her door. "I was thinking you could take a walk with me." Reaching into the glove box, I grab a flashlight.

"Is this where we take a walk in the woods and are never to be seen or heard of again?" She chuckles.

"No. You're stuck with me." Leaning in, I press my lips to hers. Dropping the flashlight to the floorboard, I place my hands on her hips and lift her from the truck.

"Really, are we going to the woods? You know what's in there, right?" She points to the thick forest behind the fire station. "And you do know it's private property?"

"Yes, we're going into the woods. Yes, I know it's private property. That's why we have to be sneaky."

"Old man Davis will have us arrested. I'll have to play innocent and tell him that you kidnapped me." She bites the inside of the cheek to keep her smile from showing.

"That's fine. I'll just tell him that it's his fault. He built that damn bridge, and it screams romance. So, the man can't blame me for wanting to take my girl there."

"Aww." She places her hand over her heart.

"Come on, you." Grabbing the flashlight, I lace her fingers through mine, and we sneak off into the woods. Fifteen minutes later, we're standing on the bridge over the small lake.

"Wow. It really is beautiful out here."

"So, you know how the story goes, right? Old man Davis built this bridge for his wife. She loved the woods and wanted to be able to explore them easily. He made that possible for her."

"He loved her."

My heart squeezes in my chest at the sight of the moon dancing across her face. I never knew that I could feel this way again. So connected to a woman. I thought when I lost Holly that I had lost my ability to feel these types of things. Laken coming into my life has proven me differently.

"I've never been here before," I confess to her.

"What? How is that possible? You had to have brought Holly here a time or two."

"No. We never did. I guess the bridge was always so hyped up, and everyone was doing it, so we just-didn't." I shrug. I'm not sure why my late wife and I never ventured to the bridge, but tonight as I stand here with Laken's back pressed to my front and my arms wrapped tight around her, I'm glad. This is a moment that I only share with her that makes all the more special.

"This is just for us," she murmurs, voicing my thoughts.

"Just for us."

I don't know how long we stand here, staring out at the moonlight dancing across the lake, but I do know that she is in my arms the entire time. When she finally turns to face me, I kiss her like my life depends on it. She is the air I need to breathe. I kiss her until we are both breathless before walking hand in hand back to my truck. When we make it back to my place, I kiss her until I can no longer keep my eyes open before holding her in my arms all night long. This is definitely a night I will never forget.

Chapter 15

LAKEN

I'M SITTING IN MY OFFICE while Jasmine handles the register and is working on putting away today's shipment. I'm supposed to be working on this month's financial report. Instead, I can't stop thinking about Grayson. I haven't seen him since he dropped me off at my place Saturday night. It's Thursday. That's five long days without him. We've been dating for a month now, and it's been the best month of my life.

I might not have laid eyes on him, but I have talked to him. He calls me every night once the girls are in bed, and we talk on the phone for hours. We're dating, but our actual dates are few and far between. That's okay, because we're getting to know one another on a deeper level.

There are also his text messages. Grabbing my phone, I pull up the one from this morning.

Grayson: *Have a great day, beautiful.*

My reply was a lame "you too." If Grayson only knew that the blush he confessed—on one of our late-night calls—he loves so much was present this morning when I read his message. Who blushes over a sweet text message? Me, I guess. I crushed on Grayson hard in high school. As an adult, I still thought he was sexy as hell, but it wasn't the same as when I was in high school. I was a young girl, and he was hands down the hottest guy in school, at least in my opinion. As an adult, he was just another gorgeous man, one who was untouchable.

It turns out I was wrong.

I would never have imagined that Grayson and I would be dating, then or now. However, when my phone rings every night at nine, I know it's him. My heart flutters in my chest, and I'm giddy to hear his voice in my ear.

I hear the chime of the door, alerting us to a customer, and even that is distracting me. I just can't seem to focus today. When I hear, "Where's Waken?" it's not just my face that lights up with a smile. My heart does as well. Harlow and Hayden Davis are a breath of fresh air and a welcome distraction from the numbers I'm supposed to be buried in at the moment.

Standing from my desk, I smile as I walk out of my office. "Waken!" the girls exclaim.

"Ladies, are you ready to pick out a book?" I ask them.

"We wanna tell you another story," Harlow says.

"Yeah. It's so good," Hayden adds.

"Hey, Jackie," I greet Grayson's mom. I try to act as I always have around her, but it's different now that I'm dating her son.

"Laken." Is it just me, or does her greeting hold something new? I'm sure it's all in my head.

"You want to join us?" I ask her.

"I think I'll find myself something to read while I'm here."

"Perfect," I tell her. "Ladies." I look down at the girls. "Shall we go to the reading corner?"

"Yay!" they cheer. Each girl takes one of my hands as they tug me to the plush green carpet.

I take a seat on the carpet, resting my back against the small array of pillows against the wall. The girls each take a side, and I'm surprised when they snuggle up against me.

"Once upon a time," Harlow starts.

"—there was a bunny and a sheep," Hayden adds.

Line by line, the girls retell their story. Well, I assume it's a retelling. They could be making it up as they go. The imagination of a child is a wonderful thing. I don't know how long we sit here, but I make sure to give them my full attention. Jasmine has the store covered, and honestly, I'm just too enthralled by the light in their eyes from creating their own story to worry about anything else.

"The end," they say together.

I clap, and they both offer me huge grins. "That was so good. I'm so proud of you. Umpff!" I say when they both attack me, wrapping their little arms around my neck. I look up to find both Jackie and Grayson sitting in the area for adults. Both of them are watching me with the twins.

"Girls, guess what?" I ask, pulling my eyes from Grayson and his mom.

"What?" They let their arms fall from my neck and watch me with anticipation. "Look." I point to Grayson, and they scream and take off running.

Grayson barely has time to stand before they launch themselves at him. I avert my gaze, giving them time to say hello. Taking my time, I stand and adjust the pillows before making my way to the register to check on Jasmine. I want to be in that back corner with them. I want to hug Grayson and feel his strong arms around me, but I hold strong. It's not my moment. It's theirs. Sure, maybe before we started dating I might have gone over to say hello, but now, well, things are different.

The bell chimes over the door, and I turn to see Lenora and my nephew, Trace. "Hey, you two," I greet them. Trace comes to me and gives me a hug.

"We were out running errands and wanted to see if you wanted to come to the park with us."

"Waken! You go to the park?" I turn to see the twins standing behind me with Grayson and his mom. I don't know which one asked the question; I struggle when I'm not looking at them.

I drop to my knees. "I do. I love going to the park."

"Daddy. Waken wikes the park," Harlow tells Grayson.

"I'm Trace. What's your name?" My nephew inserts himself into my conversation.

"My name Hayden," Hayden tells him.

"I'm Hawow. We's twins," she explains.

"Dat means we wook awike," Hayden offers helpfully.

"Daddy, can we go to the park?" Harlow asks Grayson.

"Looks like you have things handled here." Jackie smiles at her son. "Laken, I'll see you next week. Bye, ladies." She waves to Jasmine and Lenora before rushing out the door.

I give Grayson a questioning look, and he smiles. "Set-up."

"Ah."

"Yeah, apparently Mom has been indulging in the *MC Scoop* lately, and she's on board with... this." He waves between us.

"I happen to agree with her," Lenora chimes in.

"Daddy. The park?" Hayden asks.

"What do you say, ladies? You think you could use some company at the park?" Grayson asks, but his eyes are on mine.

"Actually, I just remembered I need to do... something. Can you watch Trace for me?" Lenora asks. She bends to Trace's level. "Hey, buddy. Mommy forgot about a... meeting. Is it okay if you go to the park with Aunt Laken and your new friends, Harlow and Hayden?"

"Yeah!" Trace cheers.

"Perfect. Laken, call me later, and I'll meet up with you. Have fun." She waves over her shoulder and is out the door.

I bend at the waist, placing my hands on my knees to be closer to the kids' faces. "Why don't the three of you go grab a book and hang out in the reading corner for a few minutes?" I suggest.

"Okay!" They all three race off to find a book to read.

"Grayson, I'm so sorry." I can't believe my sister did that. She could have at least been subtle about it.

He chuckles a deep throaty sound that fills my store and heightens my desire for him. This is not the time for me to be feeling... that. Not with my nephew, his daughters, and my employee here for the show.

"It's fine, Laken. My mom wasn't exactly subtle. She called me and said she had errands to run that the girls couldn't do with her. I know for a fact that it was a lie, but I didn't mind. You know why?"

"Why?" I ask as he steps closer to me.

"Because five days is way too damn long to not set my eyes on you." His voice is low, only for me, but I still glance over my shoulder to see Jasmine has moved to the front of the store, working on the display that I gave her full creativity for when she arrived earlier today.

"Sounds like you missed me, Davis." I go for playful. I hope he doesn't see how much I missed him too. I'm not even going to try and decipher why I miss him so much. The rapid beat of my heart tells me all I need to know.

"You wanna know what else I missed?"

"What's that?" I ask, gazing up at him.

"Holding you close—the feel of your lips against mine. I've been replaying our last weekend in my mind. But seeing you... it's like a kick in the gut... my need for you." He takes a step closer. "When can I see you again?"

"You tell me."

"Tonight."

"The girls?"

"Come over after they're in bed."

"You sure?"

"Yes. Nine. They're usually in bed by eight, but that gives some wiggle room in case they are fighting sleep." He steps closer, putting us to toe to toe.

"What should I bring?"

Perfect
EMBRACE

"Just you, Laken. I just need you."

"Okay." I nod.

"Now, about the park. Are you able to go now?"

"You want to go with us?" I ask him.

"I do."

"Here? In Mason Creek?" I raise an eyebrow in question, but there is a smile tilting my lips. We've tried to keep our dates on the down low, even though Tate always seems to find out.

"I have nothing to hide. Besides, it's not like people in town don't know we're dating. The cat's already out of the bag." He shrugs like it's no big thing.

"Yeah, I can go now. It's almost closing time, so we'll lock up fifteen minutes early."

"No. Don't do that. I'll go hang out with the kids. You do what you have to do, and when you close, we'll head to the park."

"Thank you. I just don't like to leave Jasmine here on her own. I know our town is safe, but I just would feel better if she's not left alone."

"That heart of yours, it's bigger than the state of Montana." He winks and heads to the back corner of the store to sit with the kids. He also leaves me swooning, wishing for time to speed up.

Twenty minutes later, Grayson and I are on foot, headed a block over to the park at the town square. The girls wanted to hold my hand, and in turn,

Trace decided the boys would stick together and reached for Grayson's.

The kids run and play while Grayson and I sit back and watch. "You know, I really want to hold your hand right now."

"Yeah?" I keep my eyes on the kids. "What's stopping you?" It's a challenge.

"My daughters." It's as if ice is thrown on our easy conversation, and my shoulders stiffen.

He moves closer. "That's not what I mean, Laken. I want to talk to them. I've never brought a woman into their lives, and fuck, I don't know. I don't know what I'm doing. We've been dating for a month, and you're all I can think about. I just don't want to bring them into this, into whatever this is with us unless I know it's the real deal."

"It's fine, Grayson. I understand. I told you. Those girls come first. I understand, and I accept that."

"Then why the stiff shoulders?" As if he needs to confirm it, his hand rests on my shoulder. He massages for a few seconds before dropping his hand back to his lap.

"Nothing. It just sounded like that would never happen, you telling the girls."

"Oh, it's going to happen. I just want us to have a little more time together. I know they're going to need to know about us. That sneaking around after bedtime and on weekends they stay with their grandparents isn't what relationships are made of. I just want a little more time."

"You have all the time you need, Grayson. I told you. I'm here when you're ready." I know this is a big deal for him, bringing me into the girls' lives as someone other than the lady who owns the bookstore.

"That's the problem. I feel like I'm ready. My heart and my body are telling me to jump into this thing with you and hope you catch me on the way down. My head, well, it's telling me I need to take a little more time, not for me, but for them."

I turn to look at him. "Then that's what we'll do." I can give him time. As long as I know that he wants this to move forward, I can be patient so that the girls are eased into this transition.

"I really want to kiss you right now."

"You can't tease me like that," I counter. The thought of just a simple kiss from this man has heat pooling between my thighs.

"Tonight."

"Tonight," I echo.

The kids play a little longer, and after they messily eat ice cream cones, we head back to the store to get our cars. Trace and I send the Davis clan on their way before heading up to my apartment to call my sister.

"Have fun?" she asks.

"We did. Trace is tuckered out. We got lucky both Hattie and Hazel were nowhere to be seen at Twisted Sisters. I was sure they would be there."

"I'm on my way. Oh, and you might want to look at the *MC Scoop*." She chuckles as the line goes dead.

Grabbing my phone, I pull up the app to see what Tate had to say this time.

More than just ice cream

Here's the scoop. Our fire chief and bookstore owner were spotted out with the littles in their lives. Ice cream and fun at the park. It looks like the relationship is blossoming.

Stay tuned for more growing details.

Tate is giving Hazel and Hattie a run for their money lately. Hell, for all I know the three of them are working together. It wouldn't surprise me the way word travels in this small town.

Chapter 16

GRAYSON

AFTER SPENDING THE AFTERNOON PLAYING with Trace at the park, the girls were exhausted. We managed to have dinner and get baths, and they were asleep almost before their head hit their pillows. That gave me time to rush and clean up the house. I loaded and unloaded the dishwasher, started laundry and folded the load that I left in the dryer, picked up the toys in the living room, and managed to look at the clock at least fifty times, maybe more.

It's been a long damn time since I've been this excited about something. The past week of talking to her on the phone each night has been great.

However, when I saw her today, I knew that would never be enough. I can't just talk to her on the phone, not when I know what it feels like to have her snuggled up in my arms. Not when I know the feel of her lips pressed to mine.

I'm straightening the pillows on the couch when my phone vibrates from its spot on the coffee table. Grabbing it, I see her name, and my heart drops. Please don't let her be canceling. She's supposed to be here any minute, and I can't come to her with the girls already in bed. Maybe I could have Ryder come and sit with them?

I'm getting ahead of myself, but I really want to see her. Opening up the message, I smile when I read it.

> **Laken:** *I'm on the front porch. I didn't want to wake the girls.*

I don't bother to text her back. Instead, I drop my phone back to the table and rush to the front door. I pull it open, and she looks up at me from where she was staring down at her phone. Reaching for her hand, I pull her inside and haul her into a hug.

"Damn, Laken, I needed this," I confess.

"You're good at hugs," she says softly.

Reluctantly, I ease away from her, and with her hand in mine, I guide her to the living room and pull her down on the couch next to me. When I say next to me, I mean right next to me. Her body is aligned with mine, and my arm is around her shoulders. "How was the rest of your night?" I ask with her settled against my chest.

"Good. Leni came to get Trace, and she brought pizza for dinner. I think it was an 'I'm sorry, but you know you love me' kind of gesture." She chuckles.

"Yeah. My mom called to see how the trip to the park went. Not that she didn't already know. You saw the newest *MC Scoop,* right?"

"I did. Tate is relentless."

"That she is." That's when it hits me. She's asked me a few times if I want to hide us, but I've never asked her what she wants. "Hey, are you okay with this? With the town knowing our business?"

"Is anyone ever okay with Tate and her column?" she asks.

"No. But I've told you that I don't want to hide you... hide us. I just need some time to tell the girls. If word gets back to them that we're together, we can tell them we're friends, and we are. It just hit me that I've never asked you if that's what you want. Do you want to hide this?"

"No." She's quick to answer. "I don't want to hide us. I like spending time with you, and I don't care who knows that. My main concern is the girls, and this being as easy for them as possible. So, if that means we have to work a little to hide this so they don't catch wind of it, I'm okay with that."

"You're amazing." I lean over and press a kiss to her temple. "Thank you for understanding and putting my girls first."

"You're a single dad, Grayson. I know those little girls come along in this package deal."

This time when my lips press to hers, I don't ask. Instead, I lean in and take what I've been craving since our date on Saturday night. I kiss her like she's the air that I breathe. I kiss her like this might be my last chance to do so. I know all too well how short life can be, and right now, right here at this moment, there is nothing else I'd rather do than kiss the hell out of Laken Abbott.

I allow myself to get lost in her. Somehow, we end up with her on my lap, straddling my thighs. I don't hate it. My hands grip her ass as she rocks against me. Her long red hair is hanging over her shoulders, hiding her face, and that's a problem for me. I want to see her face. I can tell by her breathing that she's close, and no way in hell is she going to rock her tight, light body over my cock and me not get to see her when she falls over the edge.

Reluctantly, my hands move to gather her hair and hold it away from her face. Her eyes find mine, and the hazel orbs are filled with heat, desire, and need. "Take what you need." My voice is a husky whisper, but it's all I can manage right now. My cock twitches beneath my gym shorts. It's been a long fucking time for me. I want to strip us both bare and give into this connection that passes between us. I want to slide inside her and never leave.

"Gray," she moans quietly.

I smash my lips to hers to prevent my own moan from sliding past my lips. My girls are heavy sleepers, thankfully. Those two little angels sleeping down the hall are the only reason I'm not stripping us both naked right here, right now.

"If I had more time, I'd kiss every inch of you," I say, my lips trailing down her neck.

"That. When can we do that?" she asks, making me laugh.

"Soon. I promise."

"Gray," she says, tilting her head back.

I release her hair as it hangs down her back. "Tell me what you want, Laken. Do you want to come?"

"Yes."

"Can I touch you, Laken?"

"Now. Please. Yes. Touch me now." Her eyes are closed, and her head is still tilted back. She's gorgeous.

Lucky for me, she's wearing a short pair of athletic shorts. I manage to slide my hand up the leg and slip my fingers beneath her cotton panties. "You're wet. Is this for me?" I don't know whether to look at her or at her glistening pussy that's peeking out of her tiny shorts.

"All you," she confirms.

I run my fingers through her folds, and she moans at the contact. "Open your eyes, Laken." I watch as she forces her eyes open. The heated hazel pools are practically begging for me to touch her. "I want you to keep your eyes on me."

She nods. Her tongue peeks out and licks her lips, and that reminds me of how good she tastes, so I kiss her again. I kiss her because I can. I kiss her because the thought of not doing so is just too much to fathom. My tongue slides past her lips and strokes her as I push a finger inside her.

Her hands grapple for something to hold onto, and they end up in my hair. She tugs, and I add another finger. "Gray...." she moans against my lips.

"Give it to me, Laken. I want to see you come." As if my words are tethered to a trigger inside her tight, wet pussy, her walls grip my fingers like a vise, and a deep and sexy moan from somewhere in the back of her throat falls from her lips. I don't stop fucking her with my hand until she collapses against me.

"Wow," she breathes.

My cock twitches.

"Your turn." She smiles lazily, further evidence that her orgasm left her sated.

"This was for you."

"No." She shakes her head. "That's not how this works. If we're in this together, we're together. I get to give as good as I get. Gray, I know it's been a long time for you. Let me give you this. Please?" she asks, rubbing her hand over my hard cock in my shorts.

"It's not going to take long," I confess. I don't tell her how long it's been. She knows already. Hours and hours of conversation will do that for you. I feel as though I've known her like this, not just as a neighbor or business owner in my small town. I feel as though I've known her as... mine, for a long damn time.

"The girls?" she asks.

"Sleeping, but just in case." I tap her thigh, and she stands. I was able to conceal what I was doing with her. Sure, they might have wondered why she was on my lap, but we could have come up with something. My daughters waking up and finding Laken on her knees before me with my cock in her mouth. Yeah, there's no explaining that. I'll take my chances hiding her in my bedroom.

Quietly, we make our way down the hall. I stop at the girls' bedroom door and peek in on them. They're both sleeping soundly. With her hand in mine, we walk further down the hall and push open my bedroom door. As soon as we're both inside, I close the door softly and engage the lock. I turn to face Laken to find her already on her knees before me.

"Baby...." The term of endearment falls from my lips as if she's been mine for years.

"You might want to lean against the door." She smirks up at me.

I take one step back, and my back hits the door. That's the only invitation she needs to pull my shorts to my ankles—boxer briefs and all. Her small hands wrap around my shaft, and they feel like silk. Closing my eyes, I rest my head against the door.

I can't watch her stroking me. I'm ready to blow like a cannon as it is.

"Gray?" I force my eyes open and peer down at her. "I want your eyes on me," she says, tossing my words back at me. She smiles just before she leans forward and takes my cock in her mouth.

I fight against the urge to close my eyes and just feel, but she's right to make me watch. It would have been a shame to miss this. Miss her with my cock in her mouth. She moans, and the vibration sends tingles down my spine. I fist my hands at my sides to keep from gripping her hair. I feel wild and out of control. I don't trust myself not to hurt her.

My entire body is on fire, and I know it's coming. I tap her shoulder as I hold off my orgasm, but she gives me a subtle shake of her head. Fuck me. Knowing she wants to take everything I have to give her pushes me over the edge as I come down her throat.

My chest is rising and falling as if I've just run a marathon. Laken climbs to her feet, and I tug her into my chest, hugging her tight. So damn tight, I don't want to let go. I want nothing more than to peel her out of her clothes and take her to bed. I want to explore her body. I want to fall asleep with her in my arms and wake up the same way. There are so many wants running through my mind, and they all revolve around her.

Laken.

"I should probably go."

"What? No. Don't go."

"Gray, I have to. I can't stay. Not yet. It's getting late, and I know you have to work tomorrow. You need your rest to stay safe."

I want to argue with her, but she's right. "I need to tell the girls."

"You don't have to. Take your time. This is still new."

"Are you seeing anyone else?" I don't know where the question comes from, but it's out there, and there is no taking it back.

This time it's Laken who places her hands on my cheeks and stares me in the eye. "There is no one but you, Grayson."

"Let's make this exclusive."

"Is that what you really want?"

"Right now? What I want is to strip you down and tuck you into my bed."

She smiles. "I'm not going anywhere. I can't imagine how hard this is for you. I'm okay with taking this slow."

Panic bubbles up in my chest. "That's just it. This isn't hard for me. Not with you. I can't explain it, baby, but you put me at ease, and after tonight, we know that the chemistry is there."

"Chemistry is not an issue." She shakes her head, a small smile playing on her lips.

"Say you're mine."

"I'm yours."

"Thank fuck." I kiss her slow and deep. "I want to tell them. I don't want to have to sneak around."

"Let's just see how things progress and take it from there."

"That sounds like you're not in this. I need to know that you're in this if I'm telling my daughters about us."

"Hey." She wraps her arms around my waist. "I'm in this, Grayson. Just don't rush it. I don't want you to be caught up on the high of tonight and have regrets in the light of day."

"Laken," I whisper. "I could never regret you."

"Let's just see how it all plays out. Until then, I'm yours. I'm not seeing anyone else, and I don't want to be. I want to make sure you have thought this through where the girls are concerned. We have time. This isn't a race. Not to me. I'm in for the marathon."

"Funny, you just made me feel as though I ran a marathon."

She covers her mouth to mute her laugh. "Come on, walk me out."

Quietly, I unlock my bedroom door and listen for the twins. Not a peep, so we tiptoe down the hall and to the front door. Laken gathers her purse and phone, and I walk her out to her car. As soon as we reach the driver's side door, I spin her around, press her back against the car, and kiss her with all the need and passion coursing through my veins for her.

"That's gonna make the paper," she teases.

"Good. I want the entire damn town to know you're mine."

"Goodnight, Gray."

"Night, baby."

Chapter 17

LAKEN

"SEE YOU IN THE MORNING, Laken." Jasmine waves over her shoulder as she walks out the door.

It's Friday evening, and time to call it a day. I'm starving and ready to get off my feet. The store was busier than usual this afternoon. Partly because the high school teachers mailed out the summer reading lists to the students. Luckily for me, each teacher gave me a heads-up on the books they need, and I was able to order the books the kids would need and have them in stock.

Walking to the door to lock up, my phone rings. I smile when I see Grayson's name on the screen.

Memories of last night filter through my mind. "Hey, handsome."

"Laken," he breathes. It's as if hearing my voice is a long-awaited gift he's been holding out for. It's like that every single time I talk to him. He doesn't even know it, but those little breaths are stealing my heart one at a time.

"Is everything okay?"

"Yes. I called to see what your plans were for dinner?"

"I'm not sure. I was thinking about going for a run, but I'm starving."

"I'll be there in about fifteen minutes. Does that work for you?"

"I'll be ready."

"See you soon," he says, ending the call.

I should have asked him where the girls were tonight. I know they're spending the night with his parents tomorrow night. He's already told me not to make plans. I shiver at the thought of what tomorrow night might bring.

Locking up the store, I rush upstairs and freshen up. My foot is hitting the last step when I get a text telling me he's here. Pulling open the door, I freeze when the girls start talking at once.

"Hey." I drop to my knees and give them a hug. "Now, what's going on?" I ask with a smile on my face.

"We're going to eat pizza!" Harlow cheers.

"Daddy said you're coming too, Waken," Hayden informs me.

"Surprise." Grayson grins down at us.

"Well. I love pizza, and I'm starving. Are you ready to go?" I ask, standing.

"Yes!" they cheer, and each takes one of my hands as I lead us out the door.

"It's locked," I tell Grayson over my shoulder. "You just need to pull it shut. I have my keys." When I reach the truck, I open the back door and help the girls inside. I'm impressed with the way they scurry to their seats and buckle themselves in. Closing the door, I turn to find Grayson standing with his hands shoved in his pockets, watching me.

"Is this okay?"

"What? Pizza? Of course. Who doesn't love pizza?"

"Well, that, but what I meant was dinner with the girls."

"Yes. Gray, we've talked about this. I'm ready for whatever you are."

"I'm ready." His eyes bore into mine. "I want to tell them about us tonight at dinner. I feel as though I know you just as well, if not better than I know myself. All of our talks, and then last night." He grins. "I want you, Laken. I want to hold your hand and take you to dinner with my daughters. I want them to know that you're important to me. I want you to spend the night with me. I want to hold you in my arms. I don't want a repeat of last night. I don't want you sneaking out the door like a thief in the night because we're afraid my daughters might wake up and question why you're there. I want them to know you're important to me."

"I'll follow your lead. You don't have to do this for me."

"I do have to do this. This is what will make me happy. I know you. I know you won't hurt them. I know you won't hurt me." He takes a step toward me. "You are what I want, Laken. I want my daughters to know you are special to me. Special to them. I can see it in your eyes when you're with them. They're important to you too. That means something." He takes another step closer and links his pinky around mine. "*You* mean something."

I give him a watery smile, which is all that I can manage, aside from a nod. His reply is to nod and wink. He places his hand on the small of my back and leads me to the passenger side of his truck. As soon as I'm inside, the girls begin talking a mile a minute about their day.

"And then Pap tooted!" Hayden giggles.

I glance over at Grayson, and he grins and shrugs. "Girls, I'm not sure Pap would appreciate you telling Laken that story." Grayson tries to remain serious, but he's forgetting that I can glance over and see the smile on his face.

"Oh, Daddy," Harlow chimes in. "It was so so funny. Nana waughed too."

I can tell Grayson is trying really hard not to laugh, so I veer the conversation to another subject.

"What toppings do you like on your pizza?" I ask the girls.

"I wike pepperoni," Hayden announces.

"I wike dem too," Harlow agrees.

"Really? I like pepperoni too."

"Daddy! Waken wikes our pizza," Harlow says excitedly.

"I heard that." He glances in the rearview mirror before returning his gaze back to the road.

"Billings?" I ask when he turns to head out of town. I was wondering why we didn't just walk to Sauce it Up.

"The girls like the games at the place in Billings. Besides, I don't want to spend all night talking to the people in our town when all I want to do is spend time with my girls." He glances over and winks, and I know I'm included in that statement.

The rest of the drive to Billings is the girls telling us stories and having a concert in the back seat as they sing along to the radio. They're adorable and so much fun. Grayson has done an amazing job with them, and I make a mental note to tell him that. Those little girls are happy, and that's because of the life that he's given them.

"Waken, you sit by Daddy," Harlow tells me.

"We're dis many." Hayden holds up four fingers. "We sit together," she adds.

I slide into the booth, and Grayson takes the seat next to me. He places his hand on my thigh, and I try not to let my giddiness show.

"Okay, ladies, I'm thinking pepperoni pizza and breadsticks," Grayson says, not bothering to look at the menu.

"Yes!" the girls cheer.

"What about you?" he asks, leaning his shoulder into mine.

"Sounds good to me." As soon as the words are out of my mouth, the waitress appears. Grayson orders our food, with a Dr. Pepper for him and me, and milk in cups with lids for the girls. I take note for the future.

"Waken, you like Pepper like Daddy?" Hayden asks.

I smile at her. "I do."

"How'd you know her dwink?" Harlow asks.

"Well, Laken is my girlfriend. And that means I know those kinds of things about her."

I freeze, not sure how the girls are going to take it. I didn't expect him to blurt it out like that. His thumb begins to trace circles on my thigh, and my body relaxes. I keep my eyes on the girls and their furrowed brows.

"Does that mean you kiss?" Hayden asks.

"Wike Anna and Kwistoff?" Harlow adds.

Grayson chuckles next to me. "Yes, something like that."

"Can we make bwonies again?" Hayden asks. This time her eyes are on me.

"As long as Daddy says it's okay, we can make them whenever you want." I need to make sure there is a clear line drawn that Grayson is their father, and it's still ultimately up to him. I don't really know if that's the right thing to do, but it feels like it is.

"I was thinking that Laken could start spending more time at our house with us," Grayson tells them casually.

"Oh! Can we have a sweepover?" Harlow asks.

"Pwease, Daddy," Hayden joins her.

"I don't know." He taps his index finger against his chin. "Where would she sleep?"

"Wif you. You have a bed dis big." Hayden holds her arms out wide.

Grayson looks at me, mischief dancing in his eyes. "What do you think, Laken? You think you could share a bed with me?"

I can feel my cheeks heat from the content of the conversation. Heat pools between my thighs at the thought of "sleeping" in his bed. "Do you snore?"

"Not as woud as Pap," Hayden answers for him.

"There you have it." Grayson smiles.

"I guess I could do that." I try to make it sound like an inconvenience.

"Tonight?" the girls ask in tandem.

"I don't know—" I start, but Grayson stops me.

"I think that's an excellent idea."

"Yay!" the girls cheer just as our breadsticks arrive.

Grayson and I help them put a breadstick and some sauce on their plate. The girls chatter about me staying over and how I can help their daddy make pancakes for breakfast. The entire time, Grayson has his hand on my thigh. He eats with one hand, and every time I look over at him, he's smiling.

"Daddy, can we pway games?" Hayden asks.

"Not yet, sweetheart. We have to eat our pizza first."

As if him saying it summoned our waitress, our pizza arrives, and we all dig in. The girls talk our heads off about anything and everything. They jump from one topic to another, and their smiles and giggles wrap around my heart. I know without a doubt it's going to be impossible to keep my heart from carving out a permanent spot for these two little girls and their daddy.

Grayson isn't a man to play the field. He never has been. I'm also aware I'm the first person he's dated since losing his wife, his high school sweetheart, so there is a chance that I could be a rebound, even though it's been three years. I know that, but I don't care.

I refuse to give the three of them any less than all of me. If things don't work out, then they don't work out. It's going to hurt, but heartbreak is supposed to hurt. I would much rather love them while I can and have those memories if our time together ends. Life is about risks and taking chances, and I've done very little of that until now.

I'm all in, and if I'm being honest, my heart is already invested with all three of them.

"Now?" Harlow asks.

"You each need to take one more bite, and we can go play a few games."

The girls waste no time shoving another bite of pizza into their mouths and slide out of the booth while they're still chewing, making both Grayson and me laugh at their antics.

He slides out of the booth and offers me his hand to help me out. I take it and slide out. I expect him to let go, but he doesn't. He keeps ahold of my hand as we follow the girls to a small section of arcade games. Grayson digs into his pocket for some quarters that I know he must have placed there on purpose. No man walks around with a handful of quarters in his pocket.

"I always come prepared," he says, seeing the question in my eyes.

"You're a great father, Grayson Davis."

I'm surprised when he leans down and places a quick kiss on the corner of my mouth. "Thank you. It's a guessing game on most days."

"Well, your guesses are good. They're beautiful, healthy, happy little girls. That's all on you."

He gives my hand a squeeze and turns his attention back to his daughters. They play round after round, and the entire time, Grayson holds my hand in his.

From the outside looking in, we're the perfect family. My heart squeezes at the thought of Holly missing out on her daughters growing up. I don't know where this is headed. I hope this is leading toward something lasting and permanent. I make a silent vow to make sure Harlow and Hayden know how kind and beautiful their mother was. I'll also make sure they know how much she loved them.

The drive home is quiet, and it's obvious the girls are exhausted. They're asleep before we're outside of the corporation limits of Billings.

"You're staying with me tonight, right?"

"Yes." I don't hesitate.

"You need to stop and get clothes?"

"I should get something to sleep in at least. I can come home in the morning and shower."

"How about you get something to wear tomorrow and get what you need to shower at my place?"

"I have to open the shop in the morning."

He nods. "I know, but I want you to make breakfast with us and start your day with us. Then when you close up, I want you to come home to us."

"Then, yeah, I'm going to need a few things." Everything he just said is what I want. Only, I wish I didn't have to go to work. I want to spend my morning with the three of them. I think it's time to hire more help at the bookstore. Things are going well, but I've never had much of a dating life, so I just worked the hours, saving me and the business even more money because of it. I can afford it. I want to spend time with Grayson and the girls. I'll be placing a Help Wanted sign in the front window very soon.

Chapter 18

GRAYSON

W HEN WE MADE IT BACK to my place, Laken and I both carried one of the girls inside. She helped me get them in their pajamas and coerce them to use the potty before tucking them in. It's been a long damn time since I've had help with the twins' nightly routine. If tonight has shown me anything, it's that I didn't realize how lonely I was. I've been missing the companionship that comes with a relationship.

Laken fits so well with us. She jumps right in and helps with the girls. She listens to their silly stories, and she shows them love and compassion. I never imagined sharing my life with anyone but Holly.

Life had other plans, and here I am. A single father, twin girls, and the boyfriend of a woman who blows my mind.

She's everything I want. She's everything I need. I already know I never want to let her go.

I'm not going to tell her that. She'd think I've lost my mind, and maybe I have. All I know is that she appeared in my life for a reason I can't explain, not when technically she's been there all along. Now, what I want to do is keep her close. I want to submerge her in my life and my daughters.' I want to see where this goes.

Some may say it's too soon to bring a woman into my daughters' life. We've only been dating a handful of weeks, but I'm confident this is the right thing for us.

I had the same feeling when Holly and I started dating all the way back in high school. I knew she was going to change my life. At the time, I didn't know it would be to show me love and give me a part of both of us. I didn't know when the twins were born they would be forever a piece of the two of us or that we would lose their mother when we did, when they were so young. Holly is gone, her time here on earth ended far too soon, but there is still a piece of her here. Two four-year-old pieces who are the best parts of both of us. I owe it to them to show them what it looks like for a man to love a woman.

"You ready for bed?" I ask Laken, leading her by the hand to my bedroom down the hall.

"I need to go grab my bag out of the truck."

"I'll get it. Be right back." I kiss her quickly before going to grab her bag out of my truck. She wanted to just follow me over, but it's late, and I insisted on driving. Sure, my house is a few miles at best outside of town, but that doesn't matter. I wanted her with me.

Rushing back to my room, I peek in on the girls, who are sound asleep, and then disappear behind my bedroom door. I place her bag on the floor and allow my feet to carry me to where she's sitting on the bed. Her eyes are trained on a picture of Holly and the girls sitting on the nightstand.

"She was beautiful," she whispers.

Shit. I don't know how to handle this. Do I apologize? I mean, she's my kids' mother. She left this world tragically, and I want them to know she's still a big part of our lives. "She was."

I reach for the picture and start to place it facedown, but Laken's hand on mine stops me. "Please don't." I stop my movements, my eyes finding hers. "She's their mother."

"I can move it to the living room or add it to the ones that the girls have in their room."

"Don't do that for me. We're in a different situation than most." She removes her hand from my arm and pats the bed next to me. "Grayson, I don't want you to forget her in order to be with me. I never want the girls to forget or feel as though they can't talk about her. I know that this is hard for you." She reaches over and takes my hand in hers. "I know Holly was the love of your life. I know this isn't how you had planned for your life to go. I understand that, and I don't expect you to alter your life for me. I just want a chance to be a part of it. If you think you have room for both of us?" she asks softly.

I swallow hard, trying to rid myself of the golf-ball-sized pack of emotions clogging my throat. "I miss her. Every fucking day, I miss her." I turn to face her, and she does the same. "I miss her, but I miss you too... when you're not here. I think about her less and about you more, and I hate that. I feel like I'm forgetting her and replacing her in our lives, but she's not here, Laken. She's not here, and she's not coming back. It's been three years, and I still have a pain in my chest when I think about losing her—more for my girls than for me. I have you." I smile softly. "I don't want you to replace her, but I do have room for you in here." I place my hand over my heart. "I feel so much for you. It scares me, Laken. Holly is the only woman I've ever slept with. She's the only woman other than my mom and grandma that I've ever said I love you to." I pause, taking a deep breath, preparing myself for the words that I'm about to say. "She's not my last for those things, Laken. That might have been the plan, but such is life."

"You're always going to love her, Grayson. It's a lot for me to live up to. I know that Holly was it for you. I just hope I can bring you half of the love and joy that she did."

"That's just it. You do. My daughters, they smile brighter when you're around, and me, well, the guys have been giving me shit for weeks about the smile I can't seem to wipe off my face. It wasn't until I started spending more time with you that I realized that I could love deeply again. I realized I could feel it in the depths of my soul for more than one person."

"What are you saying?"

Placing my hands on her cheeks, I smile softly. "I'm saying that I'm falling hard and fast, Laken. I fell in love with Holly when I was a kid. We weren't perfect, but we loved each other, and we worked hard every day to nurture that love. Then I lost her. I lost myself… until you. We're not perfect, and my deceased wife will always own a part of me, but you, Laken, you own just as much of me as she did. I know that sounds crazy, but it's my tragedy and my truth."

There are tears swimming in her eyes, but she's smiling, so my guess is that they are happy tears. "I never want them to feel as though they can't talk about her when I'm around. I want them to know how amazing she was and how much she loved them. I want them to know how much you loved her."

"Can I say something else? Something that's going to make me sound like I need to be committed, but I believe it all the same?"

"You can tell me anything." Her voice is soft, and her eyes, they're looking at me with so much understanding and, dare I hope, love?

"I think she's behind this. Behind us. I don't know how else to explain the fact that we've lived in the same small town all our lives, and I'm just now noticing how amazing you are." I run my fingers through the silky strands of her hair.

"That doesn't sound crazy. Not at all. Holly was… so nice." She chuckles. "I don't know how else to explain it. If I would pass her in the grocery store or on the street, even when she came into my store, she was always so sweet. Hell, even in high school, when she caught me telling Justine how hot I thought you were, she was cool about it. Not rude or snide or bitchy."

"Wait, I think I need to hear this story."

She goes on to tell me all about that day in the bathroom sophomore year. "It was easy to see why you loved her the way that you do."

"Did."

"What?"

"You said 'do.'"

She shrugs. "You love her, Grayson. She was taken from you. You didn't stop loving her. She didn't stop loving you. What happened to Holly and her sister was tragic. I don't know all the details, but I know they are both gone way too soon."

I don't have words. Not that I could get my mouth to work to speak them if I did with the emotions rolling through my veins and wrapping themselves around my heart. Instead, I pull Laken into my lap and hold her. I sit here with my arms wrapped around this woman who is more understanding and patient than I deserve, and I know it's coming from a place of love.

"We should get ready for bed," she murmurs.

"Yes. You have to work tomorrow. What time do you need to get up, and I'll set my alarm?"

"We open at eight, so as long as I'm up around seven, I should be fine."

I release my hold on her, and she stands. "I'll be right back."

She takes her bag into my bathroom and closes the door behind her. My eyes land on the picture frame of Holly and the girls on their first birthday. She was gone a week later. "She's amazing, Holls. Thank you for sending her to me," I whisper. I know it's a crazy thing to believe, but I feel it in my soul.

A few minutes later, Laken appears, wearing a tank top and a short pair of shorts. Her hair is pulled up in a messy knot on the top of her head. She takes my breath away. I want her with an intensity I've never felt before. Not even with Holly. That tells me all I need to know.

We're on the right track.

It's scary, and there are a lot of feelings and pain, but I want to move forward. With Laken. I want a future with her and my girls.

"I'll be quick," I say, standing from the bed. I kiss her quickly before grabbing a pair of gym shorts out of my dresser and slipping into the bathroom.

We're in bed, her back to my chest, and my arms are locked around her. It feels right to have her here in my arms. Tonight has been an emotional roller coaster, but there is still something we haven't talked about—how I lost Holly. I know she knows. No one could live in this small town and not know. But I feel like she needs to hear it from me.

"Laken," I whisper.

"Yeah?"

I pull her closer, place a kiss on her shoulder, and begin to talk. "It was the week after the girls' first birthday. Holly and her sister, Heidi, drove to Bighorn Canyon. They both loved to hike, and Holly hadn't had much time to go with the girls being babies and being a stay-at-home mom." I pause, collecting my thoughts. "They decided to hike another day and drive home later that evening. It's about an hour and a half from here, an hour from Billings, not a huge drive. Heidi was driving, and I was on the phone with Holly. That's something that the masses don't know. They don't know that I was talking to my wife the night that the accident happened. They don't know that I heard her screams. That I heard the screams of my sister-in-law as metal scraped against metal."

"Oh, Grayson," Laken says as she turns in my arms. Her hand rests on my cheek, and I can tell from her tone of voice, she's upset.

"I'd just put the girls to bed and started to scream for her. She wouldn't answer me, Laken. I tried so hard to get her to talk to me, but she wouldn't. I could hear screams, and eventually, sirens. I didn't know what to do. I didn't want to hang up. Luckily we had a landline, and I called my parents and then Ryder. I told Mom to call Christine and Marty. At least that's what they tell me. I don't remember much other than pressing the phone to my ear so hard I'm surprised the phone didn't crack. I couldn't leave our babies, but she needed me. She needed me, and she was over an hour away, and I couldn't go to her." I'm fighting back the tears that threaten to fall. My throat burns with the need to let them, but I need to get through this.

I don't know why but I want her to know. I know I can trust Laken, and I feel like she needs to know this to have all of me. I need to give her this part of my life in order to give her my heart.

"I can't imagine how incredibly difficult that was for you."

"She died. That's why she wouldn't talk to me. She and Heidi both died on that stretch of highway. She was clutching her phone when they finally got to her." I lose my battle with control as my tears fall. It's been a long time since I've let myself go to that night. I've been surviving, just pushing one day at a time to raise my girls.

"I'm so sorry." She repeats the words over and over as she clings to me. Then again, I think it's me who's clinging to her. I cry for my late wife and all that she's missing with our daughters. I cry for my daughters, who will never know the incredible woman who gave them life. I cry for me and the loss of that love. It's cathartic because for all the times I've broken down, this time is different. This time I have Laken here with her arms around me. It's her perfect embrace that brings me back to now.

Back to her.

"Laken."

"I'm here."

She's comforting me for the loss of my wife, and all I want to do is tell her how much her being here means to me. I want to tell her how much *she* means to me, and suddenly, time means nothing. If I've learned anything by losing Holly, it's that tomorrow isn't guaranteed for any of us. I refuse to go another day with her, not knowing what she means to me.

"I love you." She sucks in a sharp breath but doesn't say anything. "I love you for the kind, loving woman that you are. I love you for understanding my life situation. I love you for the way you treat my daughters. I love you for your heart, and I hope like hell you'll let me love you forever."

She's quiet for far too long, and I'm ready to tell her that it's okay if she's not there yet, but I need her to know, but then she kisses me. It's just a quick peck, followed by "I love you too, Grayson." Her voice is husky from what I expect are her own tears. "I love you too," she says again.

I pull her into my embrace, as close as I can get her. My heart is full.

I will miss Holly every day of forever and will always love her, but it's Laken who I'll be growing old with.

I send up a silent prayer that that wish comes true.

Chapter 19

LAKEN

GIGGLES. LITTLE GIRL GIGGLES. IT'S not Grayson's alarm that wakes me up, but the sound of his daughters as they giggle their way into his room. I open my eyes to find two sets of green eyes so much like their father's staring back at me.

"Waken!" Their faces light up when they see me.

"Shh, Daddy's still sleeping." Carefully, I slide out from under Grayson's arm and slip out of bed. The girls each grab a hand with the intention of pulling me out of the bedroom. "Let me use the potty, and then we'll start breakfast."

"Okay. You can use ours," they offer.

"Thank you, but my stuff is here." I point to my bag. "Remember, be quiet. Daddy's still sleeping. We'll make him breakfast in bed."

"Okay," they whisper back before turning and racing out of the room, the sound of their little feet a pitter-patter on the hardwood floor.

Stepping around the bed, I turn off the alarm and see the girls only woke me up ten minutes sooner than the alarm. Slipping into the bathroom, I handle my business, wash my hands, and brush my teeth. Thankfully, my toothbrush is still sitting on the sink where I left it when I was getting ready for bed. My eyes are red from the tears I shed last night, but my smile is also present. Grayson told me he loved me.

I was speechless at first, but when I finally was able to form words, I told him I loved him too. It was a hard, emotional night, but I feel closer to him than ever. Those details of his wife's death were his to keep, yet he shared them with me. I'm not naïve enough to think that no one in town ever got word of all of the details. However, I'm glad they didn't spill them. It's good to know that even Tate, the town gossip, has some compassion when it comes to the situation. That was three years ago, and Tate would have just been graduating from high school. Maybe she hadn't started the blog yet? I'm not sure, but either way, I'm glad the details were never leaked.

Quietly, I step out of the bathroom. Grayson is still sleeping peacefully. I want to crawl back into bed and cuddle with him, but I have two little girls who are eager to make breakfast with me. That trumps cuddle time.

When I make it to the kitchen, the girls are both sitting on the island. "How did you two monkeys get up there?"

"The chairs," they say together.

"You know you need to be careful so you don't fall."

"We know," they reply.

"All right, so pancakes. Let's do this, ladies."

The girls are rather helpful when it comes to reminding me where everything we need is in the kitchen. Luckily, I find a box of pancake mix, and they so helpfully told me that their daddy doesn't make them with lots of stuff like their Nana. I'm assuming that means that either Jackie or Christine, possibly both, make the pancakes from scratch. I'm with Grayson. Let's go with quick, easy, and delicious.

Twenty minutes later, and in a super messy kitchen, we have a large stack of pancakes. "Those look great." Grayson's deep voice startles the girls and me.

"Daddy, yous posta be seeping," Harlow scolds him.

"I'm sorry. I had to come and see my girls." His eyes find mine, and the heat that I see pools between my thighs.

"Well, come grab a plate. We're ready to eat."

He steps further into the room. He gives each of the girls a hug and a kiss before moving to me. He stands behind me, wrapping his arms around my waist. "Morning, baby," he whispers huskily, placing a kiss on my cheek.

"Morning," I reply, my eyes darting to the girls. They don't seem to be the least bit fazed by their dad's display of affection toward me.

Grayson moves to grab two plates, making one for each of the girls and sliding them across the island where they're now sitting in the chairs. He's taking care of the girls, so I take care of him, making him a plate piled high with pancakes and sliding them toward him.

His eyes soften. "Thanks, babe." He pulls the plate toward where he plans on sitting on the chair next to Harlow, which leaves the one next to Hayden open for me.

"What's everyone want to drink?" I ask.

"I can get it," Grayson says, but I wave him off.

"I'm already up. Ladies?" I ask.

"Miwk, pwease," they reply. I raise my eyebrows at Grayson in question.

"Milk, pwease," he says, mocking the girls, making them laugh.

"Coming right up." I find two cups with straws for the girls and fill them up. I grab a glass for Grayson and me as well.

"Let me help." He appears beside me. He kisses me quickly on the lips. "I'm glad you're here."

"To make you breakfast," I tease.

"That too, but I was talking about you healing my heart." He winks and takes the girls' drinks to them.

I stand with a glass of milk in each hand and feel as though my legs are a wobbly mess. Grayson Davis is the sweetest man, and his words easily bring me to my knees. What is it my sister said… he gives all new meaning to swoon? She has no idea.

"Waken, we did good," Harlow says, shoving a big bite of pancake into her mouth.

"We did? Well, I need to try them." I manage to make my way to the island, stopping by Grayson to hand him his glass before taking my seat next to Hayden. "You're right. These are good," I say enthusiastically after taking a bite. The four of us talk about pancakes as the girls tell Grayson about how I let them mix the batter and help measure.

"Waken, can we go to the pawk?" Hayden asks.

"I'm sorry, sweetie. I have to go to work today."

"Aww." Her shoulders slump.

I'm definitely putting that Help Wanted sign in the window when I get to the store today. "I'm sorry. We can go another time."

"Babe, you close at one, right?" Grayson asks.

"Yes."

"What if the girls and I meet you at the store, and we can walk over to the park and get some ice cream?"

"Oh, Waken, we wove ice cweam," Harlow reminds me.

"How can I say no to that?" I ask them.

"That's what I was hoping." Grayson winks as he stands. "Girls, go up to your room and pick out your clothes for the day, and you need to brush your teeth."

"Waken, can you bwaid our hair?" Hayden asks.

"Sure, if you run and get ready. I'll do it before I leave." I don't know that I'll have the time, but being a few minutes later never hurt anyone. I'll just call Jasmine on my way and let her know I'm running behind. Seeing the smile on those little faces is worth a few missed customers.

"You don't have to," Grayson tells me, knowing I have to be at the store at eight.

"It's fine. I'll call Jasmine and let her know I'm running late. It's worth it to see the smile on their faces." I voice my earlier thoughts.

"Come here." He reaches for me, sliding an arm around my waist. He hugs me tight and presses his lips to the top of my head. When he pulls back, one hand grips my hip while the other slides behind my neck. "I love you."

My eyes mist with tears.

"Last night wasn't due to a moment of emotional overload. I meant it." He kisses me sweetly before releasing me. "Now, go get ready while I wrangle the girls."

After the world's fastest shower, I'm packing up my bag and double-checking I have everything. I opted not to wash my hair, which saved me time in blow drying, so I have just enough time to braid the girls' hair and get my ass to the store.

"You can leave that," Grayson says from behind me.

"It's fine. I didn't wash my hair, so I have time."

"No, I mean you're coming back tonight," he reminds me.

"I told you I would."

"Good. The girls are staying with Mom and Dad. No, it's not so that we can have time together. It's something they do every other weekend. One with my parents, and one weekend with Holly's. It's something my parents and Holly's planned to give me time. Being a single dad of twins is hard. I fought them for a year before I finally gave in, and now it's something that the girls look forward to. I won't take that away from them."

"I only brought clothes for one night." I wasn't thinking clearly. I was nervous about staying over when the girls were home.

"Then leave that and bring more."

"Or I can take my bag home and get new clothes and bring it back."

"But then your stuff won't be here."

"Because I don't live here." My heart is pounding. I don't think this conversation is going there, but still, the thought of being here with him and the girls all the time is something I didn't realize I wanted, not until this minute.

Yeah, I want to spend more time with them, but living here... That's an all-new level. One I didn't know I was ready for.

"I like your stuff being here. It means you're coming back."

"I don't need to leave my things here for me to want to come back. Have you seen you?" I ask, teasing. "And those two littles in the living room? It's going to take an army to keep me away from the three of you." Throwing my bag over my shoulder, I kiss him just under his chin and make my way to the living room.

"Waken!" the girls call out excitedly.

"We gots the spway," Harlow tells me.

"And the bwush and holders." Hayden holds them up to show me.

"Well, we better get to work." I sit on the couch, and Hayden settles in front of me on the floor. She sits as still as a statue as I spray the detangler and brush her hair before putting it in a quick French braid. I repeat the same process with Harlow, who also sits still.

"They never sit that still for me," Grayson comments.

"Daddy, it's Waken," Hayden says with so much sass for a four-year-old.

"Yeah, Waken doesn't pull," Harlow adds.

"Her bwaids are better," Hayden adds.

"Hey, I'm a man. I do what I can," he tells them. His eyes meet mine. "I learned from a YouTube video, and they're not wrong. Yours looks much better."

"Well, it helps when they sit still. Maybe the next time Daddy tries to braid your hair, you can sit still for him as you did for me?" I suggest to the girls. They immediately nod.

"Girls, give Laken a hug. It's time for her to go to work."

The twins come rushing toward me. They both climb up on the couch next to me, one on either side, and sandwich me into a hug.

"You give the best hugs. I'm going to have a great day starting off with a twin hug," I tell them, making them giggle.

"Girls, I'm going to walk Laken out to her car. Stay inside." Grayson points to them. "Stay out of trouble." The girls nod and rush down the hall to their room. "I'm telling you their bedroom will be destroyed by the time I get back inside."

"They are two little balls of energy, that's for sure."

He picks my bag up from the floor and laces his fingers through mine as he walks me out to my car. "So, we'll be there around one."

"Sounds like a plan."

He leans in close and kisses me. "Have a great day, baby."

"You too. I'll see you soon."

He pulls open my car door, and I climb inside. Before closing the door, he leans in close. "Buckle up. Text me when you get there." His words may sound overprotective since it's maybe a five-mile drive, but after his confession last night, I understand his need to know I'm safe.

"Of course." I pull my seat belt into place.

"I love you," he says huskily, pressing his lips to mine.

"I love you," I reply as he pulls away and stands to his full height, closing my door.

Last night wasn't at all what I expected. It was more. I can't wait to see what the future holds for the four of us.

This latest from the MC Scoop

Rumor has it that Grayken were spotted having a sleepover with the littles in their lives.

Love is in the air for these two.

Stay tuned.

Chapter 20

GRAYSON

I THINK THE ENTIRE DAMN town decided to be out and about today—specifically at fountain square. Laken and I have been here long enough to get the girls ice cream and find a bench to take a seat, and already all eyes are on us. Not that I mind. In fact, I expected it. I love this town, but the meddling is out of control. Hazel and Hattie were working the counter when we ordered our ice cream. I don't know their favorite means of spreading gossip, but I'm certain the rumor mill is already spinning.

"Waken, help." Harlow lifts her cone that's dripping down her hand. I lean forward to pull the wad of napkins I shoved in there, but Laken has it under control. She reaches down into her purse and pulls out a small pack of baby wipes. She has one out, and Harlow cleaned up in no time. She even managed to hold onto her own cone and lick Harlow's down to catch all the melted parts so it will no longer drip.

My cock swells as I watch her tongue dart out and catch the melted dessert. Harlow and Hayden giggle as she makes funny faces at them. She's incredible with them, and they adore her. This moment just makes me love her even more. It also makes me happy that I told the girls about us. I couldn't hide this anymore.

"Baby wipes?" I ask with a raised brow once she has Harlow and Hayden both cleaned up.

She shrugs. "It's what Leni does with Trace. I just thought I'd grab some for my purse just in case."

"Thank you for taking such good care of us."

"Well, look who we have here." I turn to see Christine and Marty standing before us.

"Nana!" Hayden cheers.

"Pap!" Harlow echoes.

"That looks yummy," she tells them.

"It's so yummy. Waken had to help us," Harlow tells her.

I'm on high alert. I'm not sure how my late wife's parents are going to take the four of us together. I know they read the *MC Scoop,* but neither has mentioned Laken to me. I won't let them hurt her.

"That was very nice of her," Christine says. "Laken, how are you?" she says politely.

"I'm well. You?" Laken asks.

"Oh, we were just out enjoying this nice weather when we saw the four of you. We wanted to stop and say hello."

"Are you girls ready for our sleepover?" Marty asks the girls.

"Can Waken come?" Hayden asks.

"Yeah, we wike sweepovers wif Waken," Harlow agrees.

I look over at my girl and see her face almost as red as that gorgeous hair on her head, and me, well, I'm smirking. I can't help it. I'm happy. She makes me happy. She makes my girls happy.

Christine winks at Laken. "How about we let Laken stay with Daddy? He might get lonely while you're gone."

Harlow turns to Laken. "Waken, you stay wif daddy, okay?" she asks.

Anyone watching can see the moment when Laken relaxes. She pulls Harlow into a hug. "I promise, sweet girl," she says softly.

"Hey, I want a Waken hug. Dems da bestest." Hayden slides off the bench and hugs Laken, dripping ice cream on her leg. "Oh, no!" Hayden covers her mouth.

"Hey, it's a little ice cream. No big deal." Laken grabs the wipes from her purse and quickly cleans

up her leg. "Are you ladies finished?" she asks my girls. It's almost as if she's forgotten that Holly's parents are standing there. She's only worried about my daughters and what they need.

The girls nod. Laken takes their cones and tosses them in the trash can beside her. She then takes out more wipes and cleans them up. The three of them are laughing and chatting in their own little world.

It takes extreme effort, but I pull my eyes from the three of them to look at Marty and Christine. Marty gives me a nod as he swallows hard, and Christine, well, she has tears in her eyes and a smile on her face. That's enough for me to know that they approve. Not that I need their approval, but I know that it's going to make my life with Laken a hell of a lot easier if I have it.

I know I should have called them, but if I'm being honest, I didn't want to know what they thought. I didn't want to know if they disapproved, because I'm happy. I didn't want to allow anyone or anything to interfere with that.

"Laken, can you keep an eye on them for a minute?" I ask, nodding to the girls.

"Of course." She turns her attention to my daughters. "Why don't we go play on the swings?" She lifts her purse to her shoulder and takes each of my girls by the hand and leads them to the swings.

"I'm sorry," I say, as soon as they're out of earshot. "I should have told you about Laken and me, I just… I didn't want to hurt you, and I didn't want you to tell me you didn't approve of her."

"Gray," Marty says, his voice gruff. "Son, that's not for us to decide. Unless those babies are in danger, it's your decision."

"Laken is a sweet woman. She's so good with the girls." Christine smiles sadly. "She's good for them."

"She really is." I glance over to where she's pushing them on the swings. Both of the girls' laughter greets my ears, and all three of them are wearing huge smiles. "She's good for all three of us."

"Well, we'll see you in a little while. Are you still dropping them off around five?" Marty asks.

"Yes. You know they wouldn't miss one of your sleepovers."

"We love them too." He chuckles. "Keeps us young." With that, he throws his arm over his wife's shoulder and leads her in the opposite direction.

I watch them walk away before going to my girls. All three of them. "You need some help?" I ask Laken. She has her hands full, pushing both girls.

"Yes." She huffs out a laugh. "These two keep me on my toes."

"Don't I know it." We push the girls for about fifteen minutes, and they lose interest. "All right, we need to get home and get cleaned up and get your bags packed for your sleepover tonight."

"Waken, you hafta pack a bag too for your sweepover wif Daddy," Hayden reminds her.

"You're right. How about you come up to my apartment, and you and your sister can help me pack?"

"Yay!" They jump up and down with excitement.

The walk back to Laken's store is filled with chatter from the girls and lots of smiles and waves from the townspeople. I can only imagine what Tate is going to have to say about today's outing. Not that it bothers me. Laken and I are solid. Besides, Tate isn't about breaking up relationships. She is more about bringing them to the surface, helping bring people together.

"Thank you for dinner," Laken says as we make our way out of Sauce It Up, an Italian restaurant that sits behind her bookstore one block over.

"It's been a while since I've been there. It was good."

"Definitely. I can smell it from my apartment, and sometimes I can't resist ordering something and picking it up."

"You never dine in?"

"Sometimes, but never by myself. It feels weird. Besides, this town talks. I swear the walls have eyes. Can you imagine the ladies that would be trying to fix me up with their sons, or nephews, or hell, their neighbor's son?" She laughs. "I'll pass."

"Good thing you ate there with your boyfriend tonight. Wouldn't want anyone trying to take my girl."

"Trust me, Gray, you have nothing to worry about. I'm right where I want to be."

"Oh, yeah?" I ask as we approach my truck. "I have somewhere I'd like you to be."

She turns to face me. "Where's that?"

I lean in close, my lips a breath from hers. "In my bed." Placing my hands on her hips, I move her body closer to mine, and she melts against me.

"Let's do that," she says, smiling up at me.

"You sure? The night's still young."

"Take me to bed, Grayson." The words are a husky whisper from her lips.

"My pleasure." I kiss her quickly before reaching around her and pulling open my truck door for her.

"You want me to drive my car? So you don't have to take me home?"

"No. I want you with me." She nods, and I know she's picked up on this fear I have of something happening to her. It's not a constant, but anytime she talks about driving, it presents itself.

The drive to my place is short, and the anticipation of what's yet to come is coursing through my veins. I'm keyed up, and if the way her leg is bouncing is any indication, she is as well. Our relationship has been a whirlwind. We fell hard and fast. We love each other, and now we're about to take that love, take our relationship to a deeper level.

I know I'm not the normal male population, but I like the fact that the first woman I made love to ended up my wife, and now the second, well, she holds my heart now. Casual has never been my thing. I have two little girls who require me to be serious. I won't risk their hearts on a casual relationship. Before them, Holly was the only woman I could see.

Pulling into my driveway, Laken has her door open and is climbing out of the truck before I have a chance to tell her to wait for me. Springing into action, I grab my keys and follow after her. When I reach where she's standing, she holds her hand out for me, and I don't hesitate to take it. Together, we make our way into the house. We kick off our shoes, and I lock the door before I lead her blindly down the hall to my room. Thankfully there are no toy mishaps along the way. Nothing hurts worse than stepping on one of those little plastic Barbie shoes with your bare feet.

Once we're in my room, I walk to the bathroom and turn on the light, positioning the door just so there is a soft glow in the room. "I want to be able to see you," I explain when she gives me a questioning look.

"Oh, yeah? You like watching me sleep?" she teases.

"I'll do that too. After I've tasted every inch of your skin," I say, trailing kisses down her neck.

"I like this plan."

"Me too, baby. I like it a whole hell of a lot." Stepping back, I reach behind my head for the neck of my T-shirt and pull it off, letting it fall to the floor. "Your turn." I smile at her. I'd love nothing more than to strip her out of her clothes, but I know my girl, and she'd want to reciprocate, and I can't have her hands on me. Not yet. I'm barely maintaining control at the thought of her pussy gripping my cock.

"Like this?" she asks, lifting the hem of her shirt and tugging it over her head.

"Yeah," I reply, my voice thick.

I reach for the button on my shorts as she takes a step forward. "Need some help?"

"No." I huff out a laugh. "Baby, I want your hands on me. I do. But if you touch me right now, I'm going to lose it."

"You mean my hands on you are going to make you lose control?" She tilts her head to the side. "That's not a bad thing."

"It is when all I can think about is coming with your pussy gripping my cock."

Her chest rapidly rises and falls with each breath. "Yeah, we could do that too," she murmurs, licking her lips.

"Naked, baby. I need you naked." She nods and slips out of her shorts. I stand still as I watch her.

She's standing before me in nothing but a green pair of lace panties and a matching bra. I can't tell from the dim lighting, but I know that the matching set brings out the color of her eyes. Her long red hair hangs down her back, and a flash of me gripping the long locks while taking her from behind plays out like a movie reel in my mind.

"What are you thinking right now?"

"About you."

"What about me, specifically?" she asks.

"That's for another time," I tell her. I can't take her like a savage who's been deprived of pussy for far too long our first time together.

"Tell me, Grayson. No secrets, right?"

Fuck. She's got me there. I swallow hard and tell her exactly what I was thinking.

"That. Let's do that," she breathes.

"Laken, babe, we have plenty of time for that. Tonight, I want to worship you. Savor the first time I get to be inside you."

"We have all night. I ache for you, Grayson. I need you now. You can savor all you want later. Right now, I need you." She reaches behind her back and releases the clasp on her bra. My eyes track her every move as she slides the straps over her shoulders before letting the green lace fall to the floor.

"You're perfect." My voice sounds foreign even to my own ears as I fight the desire coursing through my veins. I watch with rapt attention as she slips her index fingers on either side of her tiny green lace panties and pushes them to the floor.

"Gray?" She hums. "I need you."

It's as if her words start a fire under my ass as I strip off the rest of my clothes. My hands shake as I reach for her. I slide one arm around her waist, pulling her into my embrace, and the other slips behind her neck as I crush my lips to hers.

Her naked body feels like silk pressed against mine. My hand that's holding her close slides free of her waist and travels to her pussy.

Before I can slide a finger inside her, she's stepping back. I watch as she climbs up on my bed, settles on all fours, and looks back at me. "Take me, Grayson."

"Fuck," I mutter. "I need to get you there first. You're always first."

"I'm there, Grayson. Trust me. I'm there. The way you're looking at me, I think I could come from that alone, but I don't want to. I want you inside me when I do."

"Condom," I say, more to myself than to her. Stalking to my dresser, I reach into my sock drawer and pull out the box that I bought a couple of weeks ago and tear it open.

"Sock drawer?" she questions. There's laughter in her voice. I love that even with the desire that we both feel in this moment, that we can still laugh and have fun.

"Twin daughters," I remind her, tearing open the small packet and rolling the condom over my cock.

"Good plan," she agrees.

Climbing onto the bed, I settle behind her, gripping her hips. "You sure this is what you want?"

"Now, Grayson," she playfully scolds.

With shaking hands, I align myself at her entrance and push forward. "So wet," I breathe as my cock slides in easily. "So tight." I pull out and thrust in again, my hands on her hips. "You okay, baby?"

"So good," she pants. Reaching around her body, I find her clit, and massage it with my thumb. "Gray—" She moans from somewhere deep in her throat. "Harder."

Removing my hand from her clit, I reach up and grip her hair. I tug gently, careful not to hurt her as I thrust deeper. Harder. Longer.

Over and over again, I give us both what we need.

"I feel your pussy squeezing my cock," I pant, never stopping my thrust.

"I'm... Gray!"

At the sound of my name, I lose control. One more thrust, and I still as I spill inside her. My entire body spasms as she takes all of me. I lean over, trailing kisses up her back. "I love you, Laken." My heart is full, and my body is... hers. It's as simple as that.

Pulling out of her, I strip off the condom and drop it into the trash can next to the bed. I fall to the bed, and she immediately cuddles up to my chest. "That," she pants, "*that* we have to do again."

"Give me about ten minutes," I tell her, making her laugh. I hold her tight as our breathing evens out. I know we need to get cleaned up, but I can't seem to let her go. She's brought so much to my life and to the life of my daughters. She's my second chance at love and happiness, and I'll be damned if that doesn't have a permanent smile on my face.

Chapter 21

LAKEN

I T'S SATURDAY AFTERNOON, AND I'M pulling into Grayson's driveway. The store was slow, but with the raging storms we've had today, I expected it. No one wants to be out shopping and risk getting struck by lightning. I know I wouldn't. At least I was able to get my run in this morning before the skies opened up and began to pour rain.

It's a dreary day and the perfect reason to stay inside and cuddle all day. That's our plan for this evening. Turning off the ignition, I reach into the back seat and grab my overnight bag as well as the bag of groceries I braved the storm for. We're going to make homemade pizza and cookies for dessert.

The girls love to help in the kitchen. I can't wait to tell them.

Making a mad dash for the door in the rain, I make my way to the porch. I knock on the door, but there's no answer. Trying the knob, it's locked. So I knock again. Still no answer. I can hear a commotion going on inside. Shuffling my bags to one arm, I manage to slide my phone out of my purse and hit Grayson's number.

"Laken," he greets me. Is that panic in his voice?

"Gray? What's wrong?"

"Nothing, just cleaning up a mess."

"Well, I'm at the door. Come let me in, and I'll help."

"Shit. I'm sorry. I locked it to take a shower and set the alarm since the girls were out here by themselves. I should have been more worried about locking the damn dishwasher," he mutters.

"What?"

"I'll show you."

The line goes dead, and a few seconds later, Grayson opens the front door. He's soaked. As in his clothes are drenched, and there's a frown on his face.

"What happened? Where are the girls?" I ask, stepping inside.

"The girls are on the couch in time-out. I'm in the kitchen. Follow me. It's easier to show you. You might want to kick off your shoes."

Confused as to what's going on, I do as he says, kicking off my shoes. I leave my overnight bag and my purse by the door, opting to take the groceries with me. I am going to the kitchen after all. As soon as we round the corner, I gasp. There are bubbles everywhere. *Everywhere.*

"Grayson?"

"Apparently, when I told the girls to pick up, they decided to help me clean. They did the dishes."

"Okay."

"They used dish detergent in the dishwasher. As in not dishwasher detergent," he sighs, raking his hands through his hair, leaving a trail of bubbles, making me laugh.

"It's not funny, Laken. Look at my kitchen."

"I am. I'm also looking at the bubbles you just left in your hair," I tease.

"Shit," he mutters.

"Hey." I walk into the madness and place the bag of groceries on the island. "It's okay. Sure, it's a mess we need to clean up, and hopefully there's no damage to the flooring or the cabinets, but the bright side is that the girls are safe. No one got hurt in the making of these bubbles." A smile tilts my lips.

"I installed waterproof flooring when we moved in. I figured with twins I would need it."

"See, there you go. You were thinking ahead. Grab a mop and maybe a shop vac if you have one, and we'll get this place cleaned up."

He tugs me into his arms and kisses me softly. "I love you. I'm sorry for being short."

"Life is messy, Gray. We can't control it even if we try. What we can do is embrace it and find the good." I kiss his chin. "Hey, girls, can you come in here for a minute?" I call out.

"What are you doing? We have to clean this up. They might fall."

"They're probably going to fall, Grayson, and that's okay. We're here to keep them safe. They need to help clean this up, and besides, it looks like fun."

"Fun?"

"Waken." Harlow sniffs from the doorway.

"We made a mess," Hayden says, her bottom lip jutting out.

"Come here." I crouch down and hold my arms open for them. "It was an accident," I tell them. "But we're going to help Daddy clean it up. What do you say?" They nod their little heads, sorrow still marring their features. "Daddy, grab the shop vac."

Grayson nods but doesn't make his way toward the garage. Instead, he lifts each of the twins, setting them on the counter, then pulls me to his side. I slip a little on the sudsy floor, but his grip on me is firm. "My girls," he says, gathering the three of us into a hug. I feel his lips press against my temple. "Thank you," he whispers.

"You're welcome. Now, let's get this cleaned up. I brought supplies to make cookies and homemade pizza."

"Yay!" the girls cheer.

Grayson leaves to grab the shop vac, and I place the girls back on their feet. "Have you ever skated in bubbles?" I ask them. They shake their head. "Well, let me show you." I take a few steps and then slide a little, catching myself on the counter. "Don't slide too fast so you don't fall."

The girls take off at the same time and slide into me. Their laughter is contagious. "Okay, this time we'll do it together, ready?" I ask. They nod. "Go." The three of us take off and slide to the other side of the kitchen.

"Wee!" Hayden says, taking another turn, sliding to the other side once more.

"Watch me, sissy!" Harlow calls out. She does the same, and I'm just about to call them out to watch me when Grayson's laughter catches me off guard.

"I leave you for what, two minutes max, and you've turned my sudsy kitchen into a skating rink."

"You make the best of what you're given, Gray." Something flashes in his eyes, and I'm worried I've overstepped. That is until he comes to stand beside me and pushes off the counter, sliding toward the girls. They cheer for him, and that won't do. This was my idea after all. I'm the victor here.

I take off and slide, going a little faster than I realized, and crash into Grayson, which lands us both on the floor covered in suds. The twins want in on the action, so they fall on top of us in a fit of giggles. I want to take a picture of this moment, not that I'll need it. This day will forever be in my mind.

It's not just Grayson that I love. I love his daughters too. I love the domestic picture that we create. I love that in my mind we're a family. The three of them are my family, and I couldn't love the girls more if they were my own.

And Grayson, well, he's the love of my life.

A year ago, if someone would have told me that this is where I would be, I would have laughed. Now, well, this is my life. A life I love. A life I embrace.

When we finally get our laughter under control, Gray sends the girls to change clothes, instructing them to leave the wet clothes in the tub while he uses the shop vac, and I come behind him with the mop to clean up the mess.

"Thanks for your help."

"You're welcome."

"Not just with the mess, with the girls."

"I didn't overstep?"

"No. You were great with them. You're right. Everyone was safe. I was just overwhelmed, is all."

"That's understandable, Gray. You're doing a great job with them."

"Thank you," he says, pulling me into the perfect embrace. "You are too."

"Girls, it's time for a bath, then bed," Grayson announces once the credits roll of the princess movie we were watching.

"Waken, can you give us a baf?" Harlow asks.

I look over at Grayson, and he nods and shrugs, leaving the decision up to me. "Of course," I tell her. "Go pick your jammies, and I'll be there in a minute."

They jump off the couch and rush down the hall to their room.

"Are you sure you're okay with me giving them a bath?" I ask Grayson.

"They asked for you."

I nod. "But are you okay with it?"

"I trust you with them, Laken. You're a part of our lives. Of course, I'm okay with it. I'm going to clean the kitchen from dinner, and then I'll be up to help."

I study him to see if there is any hesitation on his part. I'm in deep with all three of them, and the last thing I want to do is step on Grayson's toes or make him feel as though I'm trying to play the role of mom. Not that I would mind that. In fact, when I think about the future, it's the three of us, and I am their mother figure. It's important to me that we take this at his pace and theirs. The last thing I want is for any of them, hell any of us, to get hurt.

Slow and steady wins the race.

I find the girls in their room, pajamas in hand. "Ready, ladies?"

"Yes!" They race past me into their bathroom and begin to strip out of their clothes. I start the water and toss in some bubbles, making them giggle. By the time Grayson joins us, we're draining the water, and the girls have towels draped around their bodies.

"Just in time." I smile up at him from where I'm kneeling next to the bathtub.

He and I work together to get the girls dressed and ready for bed.

"Waken, can you bwaid our hair?" Harlow asks.

"Of course I can."

"Mine too," Hayden insists.

"Come here." I pat between my legs from my spot on Harlow's bed. She wastes no time settling in front of me, letting me get to work on braiding her hair.

"I wove bwaids," Harlow says.

"Me too," Hayden agrees.

"Well, I like braiding your hair, so I think we're even." When I finish with Harlow, she climbs onto Hayden's bed with Grayson while I braid Hayden's hair. The girls talk about how they love making pizzas and cookies, and we even laugh about the slipping and sliding we did in the bubbles.

"You're done," I tell Hayden.

"Daddy, will you wead to us?" Hayden asks.

"Yes. Get in bed, and I'll grab a book."

I stand to leave.

"Where are you going?" he asks.

"I'm just going to go get ready for bed. Give you three some time."

"You don't have to," he says quickly.

"I know." I smile at him. "Girls, can I have a goodnight hug?" Without hesitation, they wrap their arms around me one at a time. "Thank you. Those were big hugs. Goodnight, ladies." I wave and head out of their room.

"Daddy, we wove Waken," one of them says. I don't know who because I'm not looking at them, but it doesn't matter when the "Me too, Daddy" is echoed.

"I love her too," Grayson tells them. "Now, get in bed, monkeys."

I smile and retreat to his room, my heart full. I take my time brushing my teeth and getting changed for bed. Today has been the best day. I love spending time with the three of them, and I can't help but hope that this is my future. Saturday evenings at home with my family. I want them to be mine.

Turning off the bathroom light, I step into the bedroom just as Grayson enters. "Hey, are they asleep?"

"Yeah." He smiles. "Must have been all of the bubble skating." He chuckles.

"Hey, they had fun, and it turned a bad situation into a positive one."

"You are the positive in our lives. You know that, right?"

"I know that the three of you are the light in my day, my night, my week, hell my life." I smile up at him.

He snakes his arms around my waist and pulls me close. "I love you."

"I love you too. Go get ready for bed. I'm ready for some cuddle time."

"Cuddle time?"

"Yep." I grin at him.

"Baby, I'm going to cuddle the hell out of you." He winks and disappears into the bathroom.

Chapter 22

GRAYSON

S LAMMING MY OFFICE DOOR, I RUN my fingers through my hair. Today's run was heart-wrenching and so much like the tragedy of my past. It doesn't matter how much time passes. Anytime we have to respond to a vehicle crash, my muscles constrict, and my nerves are shot.

Memories of that night and the phone call. The screams. The night I lost my wife and my sister-in-law. They always come rushing back on days like today, and for the life of me, I don't know how to stop it. I don't know how not to picture them when I pull up to a scene.

Usually, when I see that those involved are okay, I can channel it to helping them. Today, however, the outcome was tragic.

Sitting in my chair, I try to get some work done, but I can't seem to focus. Maybe I should walk over and see Laken. I want to wrap my arms around her and feel her breathe against my neck. I need to know that she's alive and well. I reach for my cell phone in my pocket just as it rings. I see Mom's name and immediate worry for my daughters takes over. "Mom."

"Gray," she sighs. "The girls are sick. Started vomiting about an hour ago."

Shit. I tilt my head back, closing my eyes. "Fever?"

"No fever. I think it's just one of those twenty-four-hour things. Nancy down at the market was telling me yesterday that her grandkids just got over it. It's been going around."

"We just got back from a run. I have to file a report, and then I'll be there."

"You don't have to. Your father and I have this under control. I just know how you are and that you would want to know. Stay at the station. They're fine."

"I'll be there," I tell her, ending the call. I'll have to apologize for my shitty attitude when I get there. I never talk to my mom that way, and I never end a call hatefully. I never finish a call in haste, either, because I don't know if that's the last time I'll talk to them. Fuck. When I hit Call on her number, she answers on the first ring. "I'm sorry."

She sighs. "Grayson, you have nothing to be sorry for."

"I was short with you, and you didn't deserve that. Today has been... difficult."

"You don't have to explain. The girls are fine. You do what you have to do, and we'll be here when you're done."

"I love you, Mom."

"I know, son. I love you too. I'll see you soon." This time she ends the call.

Dropping my phone to my desk, I force myself to file the report while the incident is fresh in my mind. Forty-five minutes later, I'm a mess, but I don't let it show. All I can think about is today's accident, and the man and woman who lost their lives, and my late wife and her sister. The two incidents are twisting together, weaving, and folding, and it has my nerves on edge.

"Hey," I tell Canaan. "I'm heading out. The girls are sick. If you need me, you know where to find me. Shifts are covered, so if there's a call, you shouldn't miss me," I tell him.

"You good?" he asks.

"Fine. Just need to get to my girls."

He nods. "I'll keep you updated here if anything happens."

"Thanks, man." I slap a hand on his shoulder and head for my truck. Once I'm on the road, I slowly drive past One More Chapter, hoping to get a glimpse of Laken, but it's no use. Instead, I grab my phone so I can call her.

"Hey, handsome."

I swallow hard, the emotions of the day getting the best of me. "Hey, baby."

"What's wrong?"

"Nothing. Just a bad accident we assisted with, and it was fatal."

"Gray," she murmurs. I can hear the pain in her voice, the pain for me. It makes me feel raw, spread open emotionally.

"The girls are sick," I continue. "Mom said they're vomiting. She thinks it's a twenty-four-hour thing."

"What can I do? I'll call Mom and have her watch the store, and I'll come to help you with them."

"No. Don't do that. She says they're fine, and we don't need you getting sick."

"I don't care about me. I care about helping you and the girls."

The breath stalls in my lungs as her words sink in. She loves us. I already knew that, but today, her offer feels... different. I want to hold her close, but the guilt... the guilt eats at me. I never thought I'd love another woman other than Holly. Now, here I am, giving my heart to someone else and letting my daughters get attached to her as well. They love her too. It's all too much today.

"We're fine. I'll call you if I need you."

"You promise?"

"Promise."

"Give the girls a hug and a kiss from me?"

"You know it. I'll talk to you later."

"Grayson, I love you."

I swallow hard as the memories threaten to swallow me whole. "I love you too." Ending the call, I toss my phone in the cupholder and focus on the road. I try not to let the events of my past and the events of today distract me from driving. When I pull into my parents' driveway, I sigh with relief.

I need to see my babies.

I'm out of the truck and racing inside. I find my parents and the girls in the living room. All four of them are on the couch, the girls sitting between them, curled up with blankets.

"Daddy, we's got sick," Harlow tells me.

"Yeah, it was nasty." Hayden wrinkles her nose.

I drop to my knees in front of them, and they scramble to hug me, both at the same time. Their embrace does wonders to calm the storm raging inside me. "It looks like Nana and Pap have taken good care of you," I tell them, pulling out of the hug.

"They wove us," Harlow says.

It's a simple statement yet profound coming from a four-year-old. "They do love you very much. You know who else loves you?"

"Who?" they ask at the same time.

I point to my chest.

"Daddy," they say, giggling. It's not the same carefree giggle, but it does help to slow the rapid beat of my heart in my chest.

"You monkeys ready to go home and snuggle?"

"Is Waken coming too?" Hayden asks.

"No. Not today. It's just going to be me and my girls." I smile at them.

"Waken is a girl too, Daddy," Harlow reminds me.

I smile at her. "I know she is, but I need some daddy-daughter time. Just the three of us."

"Okay," they easily agree.

Dad helps me carry them out to my truck and get them into their car seats.

"Here." Mom hands me their backpacks. "It's been about two hours since they were sick, and they've both had some Pedialyte. I put the leftover bottle in Hayden's backpack."

"Thanks, Mom." I lean in and kiss her cheek. "Dad." I give him a nod.

"You call us if you need us," Mom insists.

"I will. Thank you."

We manage to make it home without incident. The girls insist that they can walk on their own, so I hover behind them as we make our way into the house. "Bed or couch?" I ask them. They were both almost asleep in the truck.

"Couch," they both reply.

"Get settled, and I'll grab your blankets." They both have these soft blankets they like to sleep with. My mom bought the girls them for Christmas a couple of years ago, and they've slept with them ever since.

"Here we go," I say, handing them their blankets. They've already got the television turned to cartoons, and I smile. "I'm going to go grab a couple of bowls. I'll be right back."

In the kitchen, I grab two large plastic bowls that I bought after their last stomach bug. I realized getting them to the trash can that's next to the couch was harder than it sounds. So, bowls it is, ones that can sit right next to them on the couch.

"Daddy!" I hear my name called, but by the time I'm back in the living room, Hayden has already gotten sick all over everything. And Harlow, well, she's midgag, but I don't make it to her with the bowl in time.

I fight back my own gag reflex as I fold the mess into their blankets and usher them to the bathroom.

I manage to get them both bathed and start a load of laundry without another incident. Once I have them dressed in pajamas, they settle into their beds, exhausted.

"How about Daddy reads you a story?" I ask.

"Yes, please," they say softly. My girls are never quiet and soft about anything. That's a clear indication they're not feeling well.

Just as I start to read, my phone rings in my pocket. Pulling it out, I see Laken's name. I debate on not answering, but I don't want her showing up and getting sick. "Hey, babe."

"How are they? How are you?" she rushes to ask.

"They're doing okay. Their tummies are still hurting."

"Is that Waken?" Hayden asks.

"It's Laken," I tell her.

"We want to tell her, Daddy."

"Hold on. The girls want to talk to you." I switch the call to speaker. "Laken?"

"I'm here."

"Waken, we's sick," Hayden announces.

"Oh, sweetie, I'm sorry you don't feel good. I know that your daddy is taking good care of you."

"He is. Hims gave us a baf after we puked," Harlow tells her.

"Gray?"

"Yeah?"

"Are you sure you don't need my help?"

"No. We're good. I promise."

"Well, if that changes, you know how to reach me. You need me to bring some soup or Pedialyte or medicine, or anything?" she asks.

"No, I stay stocked up just in case." It's something I've learned as a single dad, always be prepared. I don't have a partner to run to grab those things while I stay home with the girls or vice versa. I need to be prepared for anything. I learned that pretty fast.

"Okay. Well, you don't hesitate to call me if you need me."

"Thank you, Laken."

"Girls?"

"Yeah?"

"I love you. I'll see you soon."

I swallow hard at the sound of her telling my daughters that she loves them. To my knowledge, this is the first time.

"Wove you, Waken," they reply.

"I'll talk to you soon," I tell her, taking the call off speaker.

"Love you."

"Love you too." I end the call, pushing my cell back into my pocket. "Right, now it's story time."

I read them one of their favorite princess books, and by the time I'm finished, their eyes are drooping. I kiss them each on the forehead and turn off the light.

"Daddy?" I turn to see Hayden sitting up in bed. She looks over at Harlow, and she does the same. That weird twin thing that they do is on full display.

"Are you going to be sick?" I ask.

"No. But can Waken be our mommy?"

"Pwease, Daddy?" Harlow adds.

All the breath leaves my lungs, and my legs threaten to give out on me. I have to hold onto the door frame to keep from falling to the floor. I take a few deep breaths before I can compose myself to speak. "You have a mommy. She's in heaven." The words feel like sandpaper coming out of my mouth. It was never supposed to be like this. Holly was supposed to be here with me, raising our daughters.

"We know we have an angel mommy, but we want a mommy here too," Hayden explains.

"We pick Waken," Harlow informs me.

The struggle to pull air into my lungs is real— flashes of that night, the phone call, and then the accident today. I can't distinguish the two. I wasn't on the scene of Holly's accident, but I'm a firefighter, so it's not hard to imagine after seeing the car. The car that looked just like the one today. Same make, same color. I squeeze my eyes closed to get control of my emotions.

"Can Waken be our here mommy, Daddy?" Harlow asks.

I focus on deep, even breaths. I can't lose my shit in front of my daughters. I just can't. Slowly exhaling, I open my eyes. "Your mommy is in heaven with the angels. Now, it's time for you both to get some sleep."

"But—" Hayden starts.

"Enough," I snap. "Please, it's been a long day, and you're not feeling well. Daddy's really tired too. We can talk about this when you're feeling better." Not that I want to talk about it at all, but it will buy me some time to wrap my head around the conversation I'm not ready to have.

"I-I love you both," I manage to push out the words. They nod, and I can see the hurt in their eyes. I never snap at them like that. "I'm sorry, girls. I didn't mean to snap at you. I love you both so much."

"Love you, Daddy," they say in harmony, the sadness lifting from their eyes with my apology.

With that, I walk out of their room and into mine. I know I have to switch out the laundry and inspect the living room for any spots I might have missed, but I need a damn minute. Plopping down on the bed, I let my arm cover my eyes.

"What have I done?" I whisper. "Holly, I'm so sorry. I didn't mean for this to happen. I never wanted to replace you." My voice cracks, as does my heart.

I love Laken. My girls love her, and she loves us, but tonight— I didn't think about this happening. Never once did I consider the girls asking for Laken to be their new mom. I don't know how to handle this. The guilt is heavy on my chest, making it hard to breathe. My phone vibrates in my pocket, and I want to ignore it, but I know if it's my mom, she'll show up here, and I don't want to see her.

I don't want to see anyone.

Fishing it out of my pocket, I see Laken's name on the screen. A glutton for punishment, I swipe to read her message.

> **Laken:**   Call me when you can talk. I miss you.

> **Laken:**   My offer to help stands. Any hour any time.

> **Me:**   We're good. The girls are sleeping.

My phone rings, and like the fool that I am, I answer. "Hey."

"You okay?"

"Yeah, just tired."

"Anything I can do?"

"No."

"How are the girls?"

"Sleeping."

"Good."

"Hey, listen, I'm going to go. I need to clean up the mess from the latest puking event and swap out the laundry, and I'm going to try and sleep while they are sleeping."

"Good plan. I'm here if you need me. Don't hesitate to call."

"Thank you."

"I love you."

"Love you too," I say, ending the call. I hate that I was short with her, but my mind and my emotions are all over the place. My mind swirls with the events of my past, of the day, and the request of my daughters. I can't deal with any of it.

Climbing off the bed, I make my way to the living room, and luckily there's no mess. The blankets must have caught it all. I lock the door, and turn off the lights, and take the bowls to the girls' room, placing them on the beds next to them.

I watch them sleep for a few more minutes before going back to my room. I can't tell you how long I lie awake unable to shut it all off. I eventually drift off to sleep only to be woken by a nightmare.

Chapter 23

LAKEN

I T'S BEEN FOUR DAYS SINCE I've seen Grayson or the girls. When I've called to check on them, he's sounded off. I hate that he's doing this alone when I'm here to help him. I don't know how else to get through to him that I'm here for all three of them. I want to be there helping him with the girls. I've done all that I can to keep my mind occupied, and I've ran more in the last four days than I have in months. Nothing I do helps alleviate this gut feeling that he's pushing me away.

I tried calling him this morning when I knew he would have been on his way to the station, but he didn't answer. So, drastic times and all that, I call my sister.

"Morning," Lenora answers.

"Hey, what are your plans today?"

"Just organizing my life." She chuckles. "Why? What's up?"

"Would you mind coming to watch the store for me while I run to the station to see Grayson?" I ask her. Every time I go to put the Help Wanted sign up, I get distracted. I really do need to do that.

"He still acting weird?"

"I called him this morning, but he didn't answer. I know he's at the station. I can see his truck."

"You know that makes you sound like a stalker, right?" she asks.

"At this point, I feel like one. He's pushing me away, and I don't know why."

"I'll be there in twenty."

"Thank you, Leni."

"Remember this moment. I expect your firstborn to be named after me," she jokes.

"I'll see what I can do."

Her laughter fills my ears. "I'll see you soon."

I pace back and forth, waiting for Lenora to get here. I don't want to think that he's avoiding me since I know the girls have been sick, but something feels off. I feel this disconnect between us that's never been there. I just need to see him. I want to give him a hug and tell him he's not alone. Then I'll come back to work, and all will be well. I just need to see him. My phone rings, startling me.

"Morning," I greet my best friend, Justine.

"Morning. How's your week been?"

"Meh, okay, I guess. Yours?"

"Good. That's kind of why I'm calling. So, I called this photographer in Yellowstone County who does maternity shoots. She's so good that she's booked solid. I've tried to get in with her, and I've been on her waiting list. Well, one of the moms went into labor early. She's fine, the baby's healthy, and yes, I asked," she rushes to say.

"That's good," I agree.

"Yes. Anyway, her spot is available. It's tomorrow afternoon, and Tucker is whining about me driving the hour and a half on my own. Is there any way you can get coverage for the store and come with me? Please?"

"You know I will. I'm sure I can get Mom or even Leni to cover for me."

"Cover for what?" my sister asks, scaring the hell out of me.

"You said twenty minutes," I say, placing my hand over my heart.

"I was ready early." She shrugs. "What am I helping with?"

"Justine, Leni just got here. Let me talk to her, and I'll call you right back."

"Thank you!" she squeals, and the line goes dead.

"What was that about?" Lenora asks with a smile.

I tell her about Justine's call and that she was hoping that I could go with her tomorrow.

"I'll do it. Trace can either come with me or stay with Mom. In fact, I think it will do me some good. I need to decide where I'm going with my life."

"Are you sure?"

"Positive. Call her and tell her you're in."

"Thanks, Leni." I give my sister a hug before dialing Justine. "Hey, I'm covered for tomorrow. What time are we leaving?" We make plans to leave early Friday morning so that we can stop and grab breakfast. Her appointment is at noon. "I'll be at your place at eight," I tell Justine.

"Perfect. I'm so excited! I can't wait."

"Thank you for today and for tomorrow. I shouldn't be gone long."

"Take your time," Lenora says, settling on the stool behind the register. She has a copy of Lacey Black's newest romance, *Kickstart My Heart,* in her hands, and her eyes are already scanning the pages.

After crossing the street, I make my way to the side entrance of the firehouse. I don't bother knocking, knowing that the guys won't hear it. Instead, I walk inside. My eyes scan the room, and they land on Canaan and Mark sitting in the common area.

"You here to see your man?" Canaan calls out. I can't help but offer him a sad smile. A week ago, it would have been one of pure joy. Today, I'm not so sure Grayson is still my man.

"Is he busy?"

"Nope. He's holed up in his office."

"He's been surly this week. Maybe you can help us out with that," Mark says, wagging his eyebrows.

I smile at him. "I'll see what I can do." Turning, I head toward Grayson's office. It shouldn't make me feel better that he's been short with everyone, but it does. At the same time, it makes me hurt for him. Something is going on, and he's not telling me. Reaching his door, I run my fingers over the nameplate. Grayson Davis, Captain. A smile tilts my lips. I'm so proud of him for all that he's accomplished, all while raising twin daughters on his own.

Squaring my shoulders, I knock on his door.

"What?" he barks out.

Not the greeting I was expecting, then again, he doesn't know it's me. Plastering on a smile, I push open the door. "Hey, you," I greet him.

"Laken," he sighs. "What are you doing here?"

Again, not the greeting I was hoping for. "I missed you. I wanted to see how you were doing. How are the girls?"

"My daughters are fine. Feeling better."

I can't help but flinch at his tone and the "my daughters" comment. "How about I make us all dinner tonight?" I offer, trying to mask the hurt of his tone.

"Not tonight."

"Oh, okay. Well, can you tell the girls I said hi and that I miss them?"

I watch as he closes his eyes, taking a deep breath. When they open, they're staring at me, and the look on his face tells me I'm not going to like what he has to say. "Laken, I think we've moved a little fast with all of this."

My heart pounds heavily in my ears. The thunderous roar making my own voice sound foreign. "What are you trying to say, Grayson? Just spit it out." I cross my arms over my chest and will myself not to cry.

"I'm saying I need some time."

"Are you breaking up with me?" My voice cracks as I try to maintain my composure.

"No. Yes. Maybe. Fuck, I don't know, okay? I know that my daughters are my priority, and I know that my head is messed up. It's been a rough few days. I just need some time to sort through it all."

"Honesty, Grayson. That's what we said. Honesty. Tell me what this is really about?" I fire back at him—my anger pushing its way through the sadness and pain of his words.

"You want honesty? Fine, I'll give you honesty. My daughters already have a mother, but they're asking me if you can be their mommy. I love you, Laken, but I'm not trying to replace her."

"I'm not trying to replace her either," I fire back. "I would never want them to forget about her, but, Grayson, Holly's not here."

"You think I don't know that?" he screams. "You think I don't miss her every second of every fucking day? That I don't look at my daughters and wish she was here for them? I know she's not here, Laken. I live with the pain of losing her."

"Hey." Canaan sticks his head in the door. "Everything good in here?" His eyes flash to mine and widen when he sees my tears.

"Everything is just fine," I tell him. I then force my eyes back to Grayson. "Here's my honesty. I love you, and I love your daughters. I would never try to replace their mother. I made a promise to you to always remind them how wonderful she was and how much she loved them. I intended to keep that promise. I don't want to replace her, Grayson. I just want the opportunity to love the three of you." I wipe at my eyes, but it's no use as more tears race down my cheeks. "I know you're hurting. I know that something has brought this to light, and I don't know what it is. I can't help you if you don't talk to me."

"What if I don't want your help, Laken? Huh? Did you ever think of that? What if it's you who's bringing all this up? I think it's best if we take a break."

I nod, swallowing back the pain that's lodged its way into my throat. "Goodbye, Grayson," I whisper before turning to run out of his office. I don't stop when Mark calls out to me. I rush out of the building and across the street.

"Laken? Oh my God, what's going on?" Lenora asks. I collapse in her arms, and she holds me tight. "Are you hurt?" she asks.

"N-No. Just my heart."

"Oh, Laken," she sighs and holds me even tighter.

I don't know how long we stand here with me crying in her arms, but eventually, I pull away and tell her what happened.

"He's hurting, and I don't know why. I mean, I know what he said about the girls asking for me to be their mommy, but come on, he said he loved me. Wouldn't the fact that his daughters love me too make him happy?"

"I don't know, Laken. I can't imagine how hard that was for him. As a single mom, I would hope that one day a man will come along who will love Trace as much as he could if it were his blood running through his veins. However, I didn't lose his father tragically. He left us."

"I know." I dab at my eyes with a tissue. "I hurt for him and those girls. I'm pissed that he let me fall in love with the three of them only to rip it away from me."

"Give him some time. He's upset. We all say things that we don't mean when we're upset."

"I don't know, Leni. This sounded pretty final to me."

"I hate to hear that, but if that's the case, then you're going to have to figure out a way to stand, dust yourself off, and try again."

"I don't want to try again. I want them."

"I know, baby sister, I know." She hugs me tightly. "Why don't you go upstairs and lie down? I'll take care of things around here."

"You're watching the store tomorrow. I can't ask you to do it all day today too."

"You didn't ask. I volunteered. I'm here, I'm home, and my sister needs me. Let me do this. Please?"

"I love you. I've missed you so much." I hug her again as more tears fall.

"I love you too. Go, get some rest."

I nod and head up to my apartment. My heart aches. The pain of losing Grayson and the girls as part of my life is worse than I could have ever imagined. I wish I knew how to help him through his pain. I wish I knew what it would take to prove to him that I don't want to replace her in their life.

I just want a chance to be a part of it.

Chapter 29

GRAYSON

"**F**UCK!" I SCREAM, POUNDING MY fists on my desk.

"That make you feel better?" Canaan asks.

"Fuck off."

"Yeah, I think I'll stay," he says, taking the chair across from my desk. "What's going on?"

"Nothing."

"Bullshit. I walk in on you yelling at Laken, the woman you love. The same woman who has put a smile on your face and the face of your daughters' the last few months. That's not nothing, Grayson."

"Stay out of it."

"Nope. You see, that's not what friends do. We don't stay out of it. What's going on in your head, man? You just broke things off with her."

"I know what I did," I say through gritted teeth.

"Did she cheat on you?"

"No. Laken would never."

"Did she lie to you?"

"No."

"Did she steal from you?"

"No."

"Is the sex bad?"

"Enough!" I boom.

He grins. "Yeah, I didn't think so. So, what's the problem?"

I sigh, sitting back in my chair. "Nothing. We just... rolled into this thing really fast, and we need to slow it down."

"Yeah, I'm going to call bullshit on that one too."

"Leave it alone, Canaan."

"Let me ask you this, and then I'll leave it be. For now. When you look into the future in five years, who do you see standing next to you with the girls? I know you lost Holly. It was tragic, and I know if you had your choice, you wouldn't be in this situation, but you are, Grayson. Holly is gone. So tell me. Five years from now, who is it that stands next to you? How about ten? Fifteen? Twenty?"

I don't answer him because we both already know it's Laken. I loved my wife with every fiber of my being, but the love I have for Laken, it's... different. I can't explain it. I don't know if it's because I've loved and lost, or if our connection is just that much stronger, but I feel the loss of her walking out of my office, out of my life, like an elephant sitting on my chest.

"Give yourself some time to really think about what I'm asking, Grayson. Then you need to pull your head out of your ass and go get your girl."

"Are you done?" I ask him.

He raises his hand in defense and stands. "Let me know if you need help wooing your girl."

"Fuck off," I say for the second time. His laughter follows him out of my office. Burying my face in my hands, I fight off the tears that threaten to fall. I'm a mess.

I love Laken. I've given her my heart. She loves my daughters, but the guilt.... Fuck, I can't get past the guilt that threatens to strangle me.

I spend the rest of the day locked in my office. Thankfully, it was quiet, and we didn't have any runs. I don't look over at the bookstore as I pass it on my way to pick up the girls from my mom. I can't. It hurts too much to know she's in there, and I'm pushing her away. I just don't know how else to handle it. It's too much.

Ten minutes later, I'm pulling into my parents' driveway. I don't bother knocking, opting for letting myself inside.

"Daddy!" the girls call out when they see me and race toward me. "How was you day?" Harlow asks.

"It was a long day. How about you?" I ask my daughter.

"Waken is sick, Daddy. We need to take her a blankie," Hayden announces.

My eyes find my mom's. "We went for story time today, but Lenora was watching the store. She said that Laken wasn't feeling well."

"I'm sure she has a blankie of her own," I tell her.

"But, Daddy. If Waken is our new mommy, we hafta take care of her," Harlow replies.

My heart drops to my toes. "Girls, we've talked about this. Your mommy is in heaven."

"Girls, why don't we go pack up your things?" my dad suggests.

I place them on their feet, and they follow him to get their things packed up.

"Gray?" my mom says. I lift my head, not bothering to hide my tears. "Oh my, come here." She pulls me into a hug, and I fight the burn behind my eyes. "What's going on?"

Before I can tell her, Dad appears without the girls. "I distracted them with a cartoon. Start talking, son."

So I do. I tell them about the night the girls were sick dandy how they asked for Laken to be their "here" mommy. I tell them how I've avoided her this week because I can't get my head on straight, and I finish with what happened earlier.

"Do you love her, Grayson?" my dad asks.

"Yes."

"Does she love you?"

"She does."

"Is she good to your girls?"

I swallow hard. This is the hardest to admit after all that I've put her through. "She treats them as if they were her own."

"What's the problem?" he asks.

"I'm not trying to replace Holly. I would never do that."

"No one said that you were, son."

"The guilt." I rub at my chest. "I can't see past it. I never want them to forget how much Holly loved them. I want them to know how incredible she was." My voice cracks.

"Can you not do that with Laken in your life?"

"How? Tell me how, Dad? Tell me how to release this guilt, and I'll do it. I loved Holly, but Laken, it's different."

"That's because you were a boy when you fell in love with Holly. Now you're a man—a father. Of course, it's going to be different. Laken and Holly are two different people."

"I love them both. What kind of man does that make me, Dad? Huh? I'm in love with my dead wife and my girlfriend. My ex-girlfriend," I say as pain slices my heart wide open.

"Gray?" My mom speaks up. I force my eyes to hers, and she sets her phone on the table face down. "How long has it been since you've gone to see Holly?"

"A couple of months. I went the day I took Laken out on our first date. I wanted her to know."

"Did that help you?"

"It did." I nod.

"Maybe you should go back? Talk to her?"

"You know that sounds crazy, right?"

"I think it sounds like you're hurting. I think it sounds like you're letting yourself drown in sorrow and grief for moving on. Grayson, it's been over three years since you lost her. You're not doing anything wrong by moving on."

"I should go." I can't handle this. The guilt weighs heavy on my chest, and the pain in my heart, the ache from the thought of the girls replacing Holly in their lives, is crippling. Sure, I know that's now what they're doing, they're four—how could they know that their simple request would bring me to my knees?

"Why don't you let the girls stay with us? Take a drive, go to the cemetery. Take some time to breathe, son. You need time to process this."

"I haven't been with them all day," I fire back.

"And there is nothing wrong with that. They are safe, and they are loved. I'll make dinner, and you can come back and eat with us."

"You don't want them to see you upset like this. At least take a drive and compose yourself," Dad suggests.

"You're right." I nod. I've already snapped at my daughters, and that's unacceptable. They didn't do a damn thing wrong, but I still took my grief, my guilt out on them. The pain from that knowledge also sits on my shoulders like a thousand-pound weight. "I won't be gone long. I'm just going to drive around."

"We'll be here. You want some company?" Dad offers.

"No. I'm good. Thank you both. Just... take care of my girls."

"Always," they agree.

Half an hour later, I find myself pulling into the cemetery. The last time I was here, I promised I would bring the girls to visit, and I have yet to do that—just something else to add to my pile of guilt.

Climbing out of the truck, I make my way to her grave. I stop and sit on the grass, just like I do every time I'm here. "Hey, Holls." My voice cracks. "I need to start by apologizing for not bringing the girls with me. I know I promised I would bring them by soon, and well, I've yet to do that. That's on me, and I'll fix it. I promise."

Closing my eyes, I battle with my emotions. "I've made a mess of this, Holly. I don't know how it all happened, but I fell in love with Laken. The woman I told you about. She's brought light back into my life, the same one that went out when I lost you. It's not just me, but the girls too. She loves them, Holly. She's so good to them, and they love her too." I swallow hard. Once, twice, three times before finding my voice again.

"They asked me if she could be their new mommy, and I don't know how to handle that. I brought a woman into their lives, and they've fallen in love with her, and I'm sorry. I'm so damn sorry. I never want to replace you in their lives. Fuck, I don't know what I'm doing."

"Grayson?"

My eyes pop open, and I look around only to find Christine, Holly's mom, standing next to me. She takes a seat on the ground and reaches for my hand.

"How did you know I was here?"

"Your mom." She gives me a sad smile. "You know, my daughter loved you with all of her heart."

"I know." I nod. "I love her with all of mine."

"I know you did, Grayson. There isn't a doubt in my mind of the love that the two of you shared."

"I messed up," I confess. "The girls, they're asking about Laken being their new mom. I'm so sorry, Christine. I promise you I never wanted to replace Holly in their lives. Never. I would never."

"Of course not. Is that what you think? That Laken being in your lives is replacing Holly?"

"Isn't it? They asked if she could be their new mommy. That's messed up. I let that happen."

"You're right. You let a kind-hearted woman into your lives. You showed those girls that love is a beautiful thing. You showed them that even though we lose someone, it's okay to open our hearts to someone else."

"I let them fall in love with her."

"There is nothing wrong with that, Grayson." We're both quiet for a few minutes when she hands me an envelope. "I have something for you."

"What is it?"

"After the girls were born and you went back to work, your mom and me, we took turns helping Holly until she was ready to be on her own physically with the girls. One day out of the blue, she asked me if I could watch them while she went upstairs. I assumed she was going to lie down. However, a couple of hours later, she came down and handed me that envelope." She points to the white paper in my hands. "She told me that if something ever happened to her, that she wanted me to hold onto this letter. She said that when you finally found it in your heart to let someone else in to give this to you."

"What?" I manage to whisper.

"She said that there was something weighing heavy on her heart, and she needed to write it all down. I didn't ask questions. She'd just given birth to twins, and her emotions and hormones were all over the place. Instead, I took the letter and promised her that if something ever happened to her, and you found love again, that I would give it to you."

"This is from her?" My voice cracks.

"It is. I'm sorry I'm just now giving it to you. I'd forgotten about it until your mom texted me earlier. She said you were struggling with guilt and wanted to know if I might be able to talk to you, to help you through it."

"Why? You lost her too. You lost both of your daughters that night. Why would she ask that of you?" I ask, angry on her behalf.

"Because I lost both of my daughters that night. I know the pain you're going through. Marty and I both do. We miss our daughters every single day."

"Then you know I did the right thing by ending my relationship with Laken." Even as I say the words, they sting.

"No, Grayson, I don't agree with your choice. It's your choice to make, but I don't agree with it. I want you and those girls to move on. I want you to live a full, happy life. I think Laken is the one to live that life with the three of you." She leans over and places a kiss on my cheek. "Read the letter."

"Have you read it?"

"No. Those are her words to you, but I have a feeling you'll find what you need in that envelope." She stands and starts to walk away. "Grayson?" I turn to look at her. "Thank you for loving my daughter the way that you do." With that, she turns and walks away.

"Leave it to you to get the last word in," I say as I slide my finger under the lip of the envelope and pull out a handwritten letter. My heart hammers in my chest at the familiar slope of her writing. Taking a deep breath, I begin to read.

Grayson,

If you're reading this, that means that I'm no longer walking this earth. That's the only thing that could ever keep me away from you and our daughters. Today was your first day back to work, and I can't shake this feeling of what-if... What if something were to happen to me? Would you and the girls know how much I love you? Would you know that my life, our life, is amazing, and I'm grateful for every single day I got to spend with you and our babies?

So, that's why I'm writing this letter. I've loved you since I was sixteen years old, Grayson Davis, and I promise you even when my heart stops beating, I will love you. As a little girl, you dream of your prince charming. I was lucky enough to find mine at a young age. You are the best husband and father a woman could ask for.

This is really hard for me to write, but it needs to be said. Please stay with me while I get this out.

I love you. I know that you love me. You love fiercely and without apology, and it's one of the things that drew me to you in the first place. I never had to worry about you cheating or leaving me for someone else. You're loyal to a fault, and that's why I need to say this.

Grayson, I know how much you loved me. I know how much you love our daughters. You have a huge heart. Trust me, I know. You've shown it to me every single day since we were sixteen.

If you're reading this, then I know you've fallen in love again. I'm going to tell Mom to hold onto this letter until then. So, yeah, you've met someone. Let me start by saying I'm happy for you and for her. I know what it's like to be on the receiving end of your love, and I know how you make her feel. Like the sun is shining down on you no matter the temperature outside, and her heart, well, it's yours. There is no way that you would give your heart to her without her giving to you in return.

I also know that she loves our daughters. You would never let a woman into their lives who wasn't worthy of them. I also know that at some point, you're going to second-guess all of it. The love you have for this new woman, and the love she has for our daughters, and more than likely, the love they have for her.

I want you to do something for me, Grayson. I want you to embrace that love. Hold it close to your chest, and never let go. I want you to cherish it and live it every single day. I want you to reach for your second chance at happily ever after. I want you to chase it. I want you and our daughters to know what it's like to grow up in a *house where a man loves a woman. I want you to show them by example how they need to be treated. When they fall in love, I want them to say, Daddy, he loves me like you love Mom.*

Yes, "Mom" has a double meaning. They'll have two mommies to love them. One from afar and one with you, living each day. I want that for them. If I can't be there, I want the woman you love to fill my shoes. I want them to know what that's like, Grayson. And I know you. You're going to freak out if they want to call her Mom, but, Gray, it's okay. I want them to love her. I want you to love her. I don't want the three of you to feel any kind of remorse for allowing her into your hearts. I want our daughters to have moments with her that I can't be there for. I know you, and I know you will only love someone who can love our daughters like I would if I were there.

Let her love you.

Let her love them.

All I ask is that you never forget me. Make sure our daughters and the love of your life know that I'm watching over all of you. I want you to know I'm smiling down on the four of you and wishing you nothing but love and happiness.

I know this is hard, and it's killing me to write this letter. Not because every word isn't true, but because I never want to leave the three of you. However, I know that nothing is certain.

Today, when you left for work and I looked at our daughters, my heart was so full of love I thought it might burst. Then it hit me… If something ever happens to me, will they know that? Will they know that I love them, and I want love for them? So, Grayson, this is me asking you to love again.

Love for me. Love for our girls, and most of all, love for you. You have so much love in that big heart of yours. Share it with her, Grayson. Be happy.

All my love.
Always and Forever.
Holly

I'm sobbing as I fold the letter, slipping it back into the envelope. "I love you, Holls. I love her too. I pushed her away because the guilt was eating away at me, and here you are, pushing me toward her. I thank God for every day we had with you."

I stand. Kissing my fingers, I place them over her name. "I'll bring the girls by soon. I promise." A gust of wind whips through out of nowhere, and I laugh. "Yeah, I'll bring her too. If I can convince her to forgive me."

Wiping my eyes, I head to my truck. I need to hug my daughters. I need to tell them I love them and that their mommy loves them. It's been a while since we've looked at pictures, and that's exactly what we're going to do tonight. The girls need a gentle reminder of their mommy in heaven. And then tomorrow, tomorrow I grovel and plead for Laken to forgive me. I've lost one woman that I love. I'll be damned if I'm going to lose another.

Chapter 25

LAKEN

"What's wrong?" Justine asks when she opens her front door.

"What makes you think that something is wrong?"

"Well, for starters, your eyes are red and puffy." She crosses her arms over her chest, challenging me to deny it.

"Grayson and I broke up." The words feel like acid as they roll past my lips. He gave me a glimpse of what life with him and the girls could be, before tearing it all away. I thought I knew what heartbreak was, but I was wrong.

This is a pain unlike anything else.

Deep, emotional, heart-wrenching pain.

"What?"

"Come on, I can tell you on the way." She grabs her purse and a small bag that I'm sure is a change of clothes for the photo shoot today. I take the bag from her, and she sticks her tongue out at me.

"Talk," she demands once we are on the road.

I tell her everything. How Grayson started to distance himself, our fight at the station, his confession about the girls, and the fact that he said we needed a break. "I haven't heard from him since then," I say, holding up my phone. "Shit, I forgot to charge it. Oh, well, Leni knows I'm with you if she needs me," I say, dropping my phone back into my bag.

"What if Grayson calls?" she asks.

The ache in my chest intensifies. "You didn't see his face yesterday, Just. He's not going to call, at least not yet. If ever," I add. "He was torn up, but he still pushed me away."

"Not that I'm defending him, but that's a lot to process."

"I know." I heave a heavy sigh. "I know, and I want to be patient and work through it with him, but he doesn't want me. I can't make him want me."

"Do you really believe that, Laken? Do you really believe Grayson doesn't want you?"

"No. He loves me. I know he does, but it doesn't matter if he's not willing to fight for us."

"Give him some time. He'll come to his senses."

"I hope so," I say, glancing out the window. "But enough about me and my relationship woes. How excited are you for this shoot?"

"You have no idea," she gushes. "Originally, I was going to surprise Tucker, but I knew if I left town, he'd freak when he found out, so I had to tell him."

"Understandable. You are having his baby," I remind her.

"Yeah, yeah, whose side are you on anyway?" She laughs.

"Yours, always yours." I smile at my best friend. "So, have you thought about the nursery yet?" I ask.

Justine tells me all about her plans to decorate the nursery, and of course, Tucker says she's not allowed to lift a finger. I'm happy for my best friend. I'm glad to have her home, and I'm happy for the love that she's found with Tucker.

"What about here for breakfast?" she asks, pointing to a small diner in Billings. "I was going to wait until we got closer, but the baby's hungry," she explains with a smile.

"This is perfect." Together we make our way inside and settle into a small booth. The waitress is at our side in an instant, and we both order buttermilk pancakes with bacon, and a water, and orange juice.

"I have to show you my outfits," she says, pulling her phone out of her purse. She flips through what she has planned.

"Oh, I love that. You should let your hair down for that one too," I tell her.

"That's a good idea."

Our breakfast arrives, and we talk about anything and everything. Well, everything but Grayson and the girls. I'm glad, as I need a break from the torment of losing them. The worst part is that I'm still going to have to see them. I'm going to have to smile for those little girls and pretend that all is okay in our world. I don't know how I'm going to manage to not break down and cry the next time Christine or Jackie brings them into the store, but for them, I know I will. Unless— I gasp.

"What?" Justine asks. "Where did you go just now? I lost you."

"What if Grayson doesn't let the girls come back to the store?" I ask, feeling my heart crumble in my chest.

"No. He wouldn't do that."

"I never thought he would toss me to the curb either, but here I am."

"He's hurting, Laken."

"I know. I know he is. I hate this being in limbo. I mean, he broke up with me, but the pain on his face, I know he didn't want to."

"He'll realize his mistake. Give him some time to wrap his head around it all."

"You're right." I grab the bill. "You ready?"

"Yes." She smiles. After sliding out of the booth, I pay our bill even though Justine complains about it.

"I invited you."

"And you're my best friend. I needed this today. I needed a reason to drag my ass out of bed, and it's even better that I'm out of Mason Creek for the day. I needed this."

She leans into me, placing her arm around my shoulders. "Thank you for breakfast, Laken."

"You're welcome. Now, let's go take some pictures." We pile back into her car and head to Yellowstone County.

As we're pulling in, her phone rings. "Hello?" She pauses. "Yeah, we made it. All is good," she replies. "Okay, we'll be home later this afternoon." She ends the call and looks at me. "Ready?"

"Let's do this."

"I can't wait to see the prints," I tell Justine as we leave the studio. "Tucker is going to flip."

"Right? I'm not going to show him until I get them. I want to at least have that part of the surprise."

"Great idea. If you can hold out, he might use his manly persuasion on you." I laugh.

"I can't help it," she defends. "It's this thing he does with his tongue—" she starts, but my laughter cuts her off.

"I don't need the details."

"Fine," she concedes. "But trust me. His tongue has magical powers."

"Stop!" I shake my head.

"I'm starving. You good to stop and eat before we head back?"

"Yes. Why is it that pancakes never seem to stay with you? I eat them, and I'm stuffed, but then a couple of hours and I'm starving again."

"You know, you're right. That always seems to happen."

"What does the baby want for lunch?" I ask her.

"Everything," she replies as seriously as ever.

"I'm open to anything. You and the baby pick."

"Got it." She pulls out of the parking lot.

Justine chooses a food truck of all things. It turns out it was a great choice. The pulled pork sandwich hit the spot. On the drive home, we talk about pregnancy and names she and Tucker are tossing around.

I turn on my phone that's been charging and see several missed calls from Grayson. My heart swells in my chest. He's trying to reach me. Not wanting to talk to him while I'm in the car with Justine, I type out a message.

Me:	*Hey, my phone died. We're about fifteen minutes away from Mason Creek.*

His reply is immediate.

> **Grayson:** I love you, Laken.

> **Me:** I love you too.

Sliding my phone into my purse, I try to not get my hopes up that he's changed his mind. When we hit the city limits for Mason Creek, the heavy is back, but it's not as bad as it was when the day started.

Spending the day with my best friend was exactly what I needed. It also helps that I heard from Grayson, and he loves me. He and the girls need me to fight for them, and that's exactly what I plan to do. They're my family. The three of them own my heart, and I refuse to just give up. I don't want to live my life with regrets. I know that if I don't try, I'll regret it. I'll always wonder what-if.

Trouble in Paradise

Looks like our new favorite couple might be calling it quits. Hearts are breaking all over Mason Creek for the loss of Grayken.

We're cheering for you.

$$\mathcal{Chapter\ 26}$$

GRAYSON

I'M WIDE AWAKE WHEN I hear my front door open. Pulling up the security app on my phone, I see my mom and Christine's car in the driveway. After climbing out of bed, I use the restroom and throw on a shirt. I peek in on the girls who are still soundly sleeping and make my way to the kitchen. It's just before eight in the morning and my parents and my ex-in-laws have invaded my house. This is my mom's doing I'm certain.

"I should call the cops," I say in greeting.

"Oh, hush. We both have a key." Mom waves me off.

"You doing okay?" Christine asks me.

"I am."

"You look tired," Mom comments.

"I haven't been to bed yet." Technically I was in bed, but I wasn't sleeping.

"What can we do, Grayson?" my mom asks.

"You two have done so much already." I walk to Christine and wrap her in a hug. "Thank you for the letter."

"That was all Holly," she says, tears welling in her eyes.

"Mom, thank you for being you." I release Christine and pull her into a hug.

"So, you've pulled your head out of your ass then?" This from my dad who I didn't know was here.

I turn to see him and Marty carrying in two bags of groceries. "What's going on here?" I ask them. "And yeah, I've pulled my head out of my ass."

"Good. Where's Laken?" Marty asks.

"She's not here."

"Why not?" Dad asks.

"I haven't talked to her yet."

"Ha!" Mom cheers. "That's twenty." She holds her hand out to Dad.

"What?"

"I bet your mother you would have gone to Laken last night." He shrugs. "I lost."

"I had the girls."

"And?" Marty asks. "They love her as much as you do."

I nod. "I just needed some time. I felt... raw and exposed."

"All the more reason to run to the woman who makes you feel that way."

"I needed some time."

"Well, what are you waiting for? We've got the girls handled. Go get your girl," Dad tells me.

I open my mouth to argue, but I've got nothing. I know I need to talk to Laken. I let my fear and guilt push her away and was cruel to her. I know that I broke her heart, just as I broke my own.

"You all have the girls?"

"Please, do we have the girls!" Mom scoffs.

"Go, Grayson. Follow your heart," Christine says softly.

I nod before turning and racing to my room. I rush through a shower and throw on some clothes. It's Friday, and I should be at the station. Thankfully we have a lot of volunteers in our small town, and I'll just be across the street if we get a run. Quickly, I type out a message to Canaan.

> **Me:**   *I'm not going to be in today.*

> **Canaan:**   *Going to get your girl?*

Me:	*Something like that.*
Me:	*I have my cell. If we get called out, I'll be there.*
Canaan:	*We've got this covered. I'll call if we need you.*
Me:	*Thanks, man. Sorry about yesterday.*
Canaan:	*Remind me of that when I need my head pulled out of my ass.*
Me:	*LOL. Will do.*

Sliding my phone into my pocket, I make my way back to the kitchen. "The girls are still sleeping." We were up late last night going through pictures.

"That's fine. They'll wake up when they smell breakfast," Marty assures me.

"Thank you. All of you. The girls and I, we're lucky to have you. I don't know what I would have done the last three years without the four of you."

"That's what family is for, Grayson. Now, go. You have some apologies to make and a girl to woo." Christine smiles.

"I love you. All of you. Thank you," I say again, and rush out the door.

It doesn't take long to get to town. I park in front of One More Chapter and turn off the engine. I sit here for a few minutes before climbing out. Laken has every right to kick my ass to the curb, but I hope like hell she doesn't.

When I pull open the store door, the cool air conditioning hits me. "Welcome to One More Chapter," a voice that is not Laken's greets me.

"Leni?" I ask, walking up to the register.

"Hi, Grayson."

"Where's Laken?"

"Do you really care?"

I nod. "I deserve that," I admit.

"She took the day off."

"Oh, okay. I'll just go on up to see her." I move to the back of the store.

"She's not here, Grayson."

"Where is she?"

"She and Justine drove to Yellowstone County. Justine had a maternity photo shoot, and Tucker didn't want her driving up by herself."

"What?" I ask. Immediately my past comes roaring back. Holly and her sister.

A girls' trip.

The phone call.

Their screams.

The crash.

Reaching for my phone, I pull up her name, and the call goes straight to voice mail. "No. No. No." I try again. Straight to voice mail. "Laken, come on, baby," I whisper as I try her number again.

Fucking voice mail.

"Leni, call your sister."

She opens her mouth, but the look on my face stops her from saying whatever it was she was going to say. Instead, she picks up her phone and dials Laken. "Voice mail."

"No. Not again. This is not happening again," I say, my hands gripping my hair.

"Grayson, maybe you should sit down," Lenora suggests.

"Sit down? You want me to sit down? The woman I love is out there not answering her phone, and I don't know if she's safe. I don't know—" I swallow hard. "—if she's been in an accident."

Understanding flashes in her eyes. She might think that she gets it, but she has no idea. I lost the love of my life, only to realize I could love again. My heart can't take losing Laken.

I won't survive it.

"Grayson, I'm sure she's fine. I'll call Justine."

I hold my breath as she dials her phone. "Hey, you all doing okay?" she asks. "Good, Grayson is here looking for Laken." She listens to whatever Justine is saying. "Okay. Be safe," she says, ending the call. "They made it safely. They just got to the studio. They'll be home later this afternoon."

"Why didn't she answer?"

"I don't know, Grayson. Maybe she needs a minute? Did you think of that? You broke her heart, tore it to shreds when you ended things. Maybe she just wants a day with her best friend to not think about the pain?"

"I love her."

"Then prove it."

"I'm trying to. She's not answering her phone."

"Look, I'm sorry for all that you've been through. But this isn't the same thing. She's okay. I'm sure her phone just died."

"What studio?"

"What?"

"What studio?"

"I don't know, and I wouldn't tell you if I did. You're just going to have to wait until she gets home."

"Lenora." My voice sounds haunted even to my own ears.

"Grayson, you owe her today. Let her get away from the pain."

"I can't lose her."

"Then you have to fight for her."

I nod, defeated. "Can I stay?"

"Here?"

"Yes, here. I want to be here when she gets back."

"That's not until later this afternoon."

"I know, but fuck, I don't know what else to do, Leni. The last week has been pure hell. The guilt," I confess. Then I find myself talking. I tell Lenora everything. From the girls being sick, to their request for Laken to be their mommy, the fight at the station, the letter, and even this morning with my parents and Holly's arriving at my place, telling me to come and get my girl.

"She loves you. She loves your daughters."

"I know she does."

"So, tell me, Grayson. If your girls were standing here asking you if Laken could be their new mommy, how would you answer them?"

"I'd tell them that they have to ask her. It's not my choice. It's Laken's. Does she want to be that person for them? I'd like to think so, but that's not my choice."

"You know my sister well enough to know she's going to deflect that question for you to answer."

"I do." I nod. "That's when I'll ask her to love us forever. I'd ask her to marry me." That's when it hits me. I have a few hours to burn, and I know exactly how I'm going to do it. I look up to find Lenora watching me closely. "I'm going to ask her to marry me."

Her slow smile tells me she approves.

"If she comes back before I do, call me. Please."

"I will." She's quick to agree.

"Thank you!" I rush out of the store and to my truck and point it toward Billings. I need a ring and one big-ass apology.

I'm on the outskirts of town when another idea hits me. I call my mom. "Hey, Mom, I need a favor." I go on to tell her my plan, and she agrees. She and my dad, as well as Christine and Marty, will make it happen. They want this for me and the girls as much as we want it.

We want Laken. Forever.

Chapter 27

LAKEN

IT'S JUST AFTER FOUR WHEN I get back to the store. My heart sputters when I see Grayson's truck parked behind my building. Grabbing my purse and keys, I make my way inside. As soon as I push open the door, I spot Grayson sitting in a chair. He looks up, and the relief I see on his face startles me. His shoulders drop, and he expels a breath.

Before I can say hello, he's on his feet and has me in his arms. It's the perfect embrace, something that he's good at.

"I was worried," he whispers, not letting me go.

"I'm sorry, I didn't think, I-I'm sorry."

"You have nothing to be sorry for. I'm the one who's sorry. As far as the worry, I'm afraid that's never going to go away. You and the girls are just going to have to get used to it. That comes with me loving you."

Tears instantly fill my eyes. "I have to get used to it, huh?"

"I hope so. Laken, baby, I'm so sorry." He cradles my cheeks. "I was letting the guilt get to me, and that's on me. I let fear rule my heart, and I know it was wrong. Can you forgive me?"

"I love you, Grayson. Of course, I forgive you." The words are barely out of my mouth when he crushes me to his chest once more.

"Daddy?"

"Is it time?" The girls' voices reach us.

"You brought the girls?" I ask, wiping at my tears. "I know you don't want me to replace Holly, but, Grayson, I love them. I love the three of you, and I promise I'll never let them forget her. I just want the chance to love them. To love all three of you."

"Girls," Grayson calls out before placing a kiss on my lips.

"Waken!" They come running to me, and I drop to my knees to accept their hugs. "We missed you."

"I missed you too. So very much."

"We gots you pwesents," Harlow says, holding up a small gift bag with the number two on it.

"Mine says this many." Hayden holds up one finger. "You hafta open it fiwst. Right, Daddy?" She looks up at Grayson.

"That's right, sweetheart," he tells her.

"Open it." Harlow jumps up and down.

"Okay." I smile down at her. Taking the bag with the white number one on the side, I pull out the tissue paper and remove a small box with the name of the jewelry store in Billings on the outside.

"Open it," Hayden tells me.

My eyes flash to Grayson's.

"You heard the girls. Open it," he says.

I lift the lid. Inside, there is a beautiful charm bracelet. A single charm hangs off it, a small silver heart. "Thank you so much." I pull Hayden into a hug.

"Now mine," Harlow says, thrusting her gift bag with a small number two written on it.

I repeat the process, only to find two small boxes. Lifting the lid on the first one, I read the charm, and my eyes well with tears. I look up at Hayden, but I can't really see her through my tears. "Thank you," I tell her. "Grayson?"

"There's more," he tells me.

A tissue is thrust into my hands, and when I look up, I notice it's not just the four of us. My sister, Trace, our parents, along with Grayson's parents and Holly's. Standing behind them all is Tate. "What's going on? Why is Tate here?" I ask softly.

"I wanted to make sure she got all the details right."

"Grayson-," I start, but he stops me.

"You have another present to open," Grayson tells me.

"Grayson, this says *Mom*." I look at the charm nestled inside the box.

"I know." He smiles. "You have another one."

Lifting the lid on the second box from bag number two, I see there's another charm. This one holds a small charm with the word *love*. The *O* seems to be a small diamond from the way it sparkles.

"The girls' birthstone," Grayson explains. I cover my mouth as a sob breaks free from my chest.

"Gray—" I start but stop. I can't seem to find the words. I close my eyes and take a deep breath as I try to decipher what this means. My heart is afraid to hope it means that they're mine—all three of them.

"Waken, Daddy said that if you said yes, you could be our mommy," Harlow says.

"Yeah, our *here* mommy. We have one who is an angel alweady," Hayden adds.

I look down at the girls only to find Grayson kneeling before me, holding the most gorgeous ring I've ever seen.

"Laken. We love you. We want to spend the rest of our lives loving you. Will you do me the incredible honor of being my wife?"

"And our mommy," the girls add in unison.

I pull the girls into my arms. "I love you so much," I tell them.

"We wove you too," they reply.

"Baby?" Grayson asks.

"Baby?" the girls ask.

"Oh, can we have a baby bwother?" Harlow asks.

"And a sister," Hayden adds.

"Girls." Grayson huffs out a laugh. "We have to get her to marry me first."

"Waken! You hafta say yes. Then we can call you Mommy, and we can have a bwother," Harlow tells me.

"And a sister. Oh, pwease," Hayden chimes in.

"Yes." I nod. Tears stream down my face. "Yes, I'll be your here mommy, and I'll marry your daddy." My heart is full of love and feels as though it could burst from my chest at any moment.

Grayson kisses me hard. A throat clearing has him pulling away and sliding the ring on my finger.

"When do we get a bwother?"

"No, a sister?" the girls ask, making us all laugh.

"I love you," Grayson says against my lips.

EMBRACE

"I love you too." The words are barely out of my mouth before the girls are piling on us and yelling out, "Group hug!" It's the best hug I've ever received.

I used to think that Grayson gave the best hugs, and he does, but nothing beats the hugs of Grayson and our girls.

This right here is definitely the perfect embrace.

Epilogue

GRAYSON

Five years later

"**I** CAN'T BELIEVE THEY'RE NINE," my wife says as she settles next to me on the chaise lounge on the back deck.

Our twin daughters turn nine today, and they're currently in the yard with their three-year-old brother, Kaden. They mother him to death, but he loves all of their attention.

"Come here." I pull her into my arms. She's holding our baby girl, Ella, who just turned nine months old. "Thank you for this life," I say, holding her and our daughter close.

"You mean two more mouths to feed, a bigger mortgage payment, and a lot more stress," she jokes.

"No. For being such an incredible mother to all four of our children," I tell her.

Incredible really isn't a strong enough description. She has patience with all four of them. She manages to work and watch the two littles and the twins after school. Our moms help, but it was important to Laken, so we hired additional help, finally, something she'd been talking about for ages, and that gives her the freedom to be close to the store and raise our children. Her apartment above the store works perfectly as a nap area for the kids and a place for the twins to eat a snack and do homework after school.

"The girls got their wish: a brother and a sister." She laughs.

"And we got you," I say, kissing her temple. She releases a contented sigh and snuggles closer.

"I should start putting out the food. Everyone will be here soon."

"You need some help?"

"No, just watch the kids."

"Come to Daddy," I say, reaching for Ella. She comes to me easily, and why wouldn't she? She's daddy's girl. Our son, on the other hand, he's a momma's boy, through and through. He's three and thinks his momma walks on water, and I wouldn't have it any other way.

Five years ago, I almost lost the chance to have this: a wife and two more kids to love. I still feel as though Holly brought Laken into our lives. She knew what we needed before I did. She knew Laken would love our daughters and me and that she would be able to bring joy into our lives again.

I like to believe she's smiling down at us and is happy about the life we're living. I know she's proud of the girls and the way that they're thriving. Laken is a huge part of the reason they're thriving. She's giving them all the love and advice that only a mother can give as they become young ladies. I can't count how many times I've walked in on the three of them sifting through old pictures. Even mine and Holly's wedding photos. Laken insisted we keep every single photographic memory. She said the girls would want them someday.

She talks about Holly as if she was her best friend when the truth is she barely knew her. That's not what matters. She's keeping her memory alive for our daughters. Each day I think that I can't love Laken more, and she does something that proves me wrong.

Yesterday, we went to the cemetery—all six of us. Kaden even calls Holly "Mommy in heaven." just like the twins, and Laken just smiles at them. Not an ounce of jealousy from my incredible loving wife.

"Dad!" one of the girls calls out as the three kids come rushing up onto the deck.

"Is it time for cake?" Harlow asks.

"And presents?" Hayden adds.

"Almost. Why don't we go inside and see if your mom needs any help?"

"Okay." The girls take off with their little brother on their heels.

"What do you think, Ella? Should we go help Momma?" I stand and make my way into the house. Laken is standing in the kitchen with our three older kids wrapped around her in a hug, and I feel a tug on my heart.

I love her more today than I did yesterday.

LAKEN

T ODAY WAS A GOOD DAY. The girls got to celebrate their ninth birthday with our friends and family. My heart swells every time I look at them. They're growing up so fast. I want time to stop moving. They will forever be the two adorable four-year-old girls who stole my heart, right along with their father.

"Mom!" Harlow comes rushing into the kitchen, where I just finished loading the dishwasher.

"What's wrong?"

"Nothing," Hayden says, entering the room.

"We have a surprise for you," they say in unison.

"It's your birthday," I remind them.

"We know."

"Where's your dad?"

"He's in the living room with Kaden and Ella."

"Okay. I'll be right there." I finish wiping off the counter, dry my hands, and find my way to the living room. I'm shocked to see everyone is still here. "Oh, hi." I smile brightly. "I'm sorry. I thought when you all said goodbye, that meant you were leaving," I say with a laugh.

"Come here, baby." Grayson holds his hand out for me, and of course, I take it. I would follow my husband anywhere.

"What's going on?" I look to Lenora, who is holding Ella, and she shrugs. The smug look on her face tells me she knows exactly what's going on.

"Gray?"

"I love you."

"I love you too."

"The girls have something for you."

I turn to look at our daughters. "So," Harlow says with all of her nine-year-old maturity. I swear she's nine going on nineteen. They both are.

"We went to Dad with an idea," Hayden adds.

"Okay."

"We won't be mad if you don't want to. Dad said you would be happy, and we hope that you are," Harlow tells me.

"No pressure," Hayden adds.

"Girls, what's going on?"

They nod to one another and pick up an envelope off the table. Each girl holds onto one side as they hand it to me. "Open it," they say.

Lifting the tab on the manila envelope, I pull out the contents and start to skim the document. I see the word *adoption,* and I freeze. "What?" I whisper the words.

"We love you," Hayden tells me.

"We want to make it official," Harlow explains.

"Gray?"

"You're already their mom, Laken. This just makes it official in the eyes of the law. It's something I've been thinking about for a while now but didn't want to pressure the girls. They came to me, and I knew it was time."

"This real?"

"Yes!" The twins laugh.

"Come here." I pull them to me and crush them in a hug. "I love you both so much. I love you, and your mom in heaven loves you. Never forget that."

"Will you sign them?" Harlow asks.

"Anybody got a pen?" I ask, and the room erupts in laughter.

"Here." Christine steps forward with tears in her eyes. "Thank you for loving them. I know Holly would be proud."

"Thank you," I tell her, tears streaming down my face. Sitting down on the couch, I pull the coffee table close and sign my name beside all of the yellow tabs. My heart races, and it's taking extreme effort to not show the slight tremble in my hand as I sign the papers. I slide the papers back into the envelope and hand them to Grayson.

I didn't need these papers to know that the twins are my daughters, but to know they wanted me to have them, well, that leaves me speechless as I swallow back the love I have for them that's clogging my throat.

"Group hug!" the twins call out. Grayson grabs Ella from Lenora, and Kaden follows his sisters as they wrap their arms around my waist. Grayson joins us, kissing me on the temple.

We stand in a huge circle in our living room, and once again, Grayson and the girls give me the perfect embrace.

Thank you for taking the time to read
Perfect Embrace.

Next in the series is ***Perfect Kiss***
Available on July 29, 2021.

Never miss a new release:
Newsletter Sign-up - kayleeryan.com/
Be the first to hear about free content, new
releases, cover reveals, sales, and more.

Discover more about Kaylee's books at
kayleeryan.com/all-books/

Start the Riggins Brothers Series for FREE.

Download Play by Play here
kayleeryan.com/books/play-by-play/

Contact Kaylee Ryan:

kayleeryan.com

Perfect Risk – C.A. Harms

Perfect Song – Lauren Runrow

Perfect Love – A.M. Hargrove

Perfect Night – Terri E. Laine

Perfect Tragedy – Jennifer Miller

Perfect Escape – Cary hart

Perfect Summer – Bethany Lopez

Perfect Embrace – Kaylee Ryan

Perfect Kiss – Lacey Black

Perfect Mess – Fabiola Francisco

Perfect Excuse – A.D. Justice

Perfect Secret – Molly McLain

KAYLEE RYAN

With You Series:

Anywhere with You | More with You

Everything with You

Soul Serenade Series:

Emphatic | Assured | Definite | Insistent

Southern Heart Series:

Southern Pleasure | Southern Desire

Southern Attraction | Southern Devotion

Unexpected Arrivals Series

Unexpected Reality |Unexpected Fight

Unexpected Fall | Unexpected Bond

Unexpected Odds

Riggins Brothers Series:

Play by Play | Layer by Layer | Piece by Piece
Kiss by Kiss | Touch by Touch

Standalone Titles:

Tempting Tatum | Unwrapping Tatum | Levitate
Just Say When | I Just Want You
Reminding Avery | Hey, Whiskey
Pull You Through | Beyond the Bases | Remedy
The Difference | Trust the Push | Forever After All

Entangled Hearts Duet:

Agony | Bliss

Cocky Hero Club:

Lucky Bastard

Box Sets:

Series Starter—Kaylee Ryan

Co-written with Lacey Black:

Fair Lakes Series:

It's Not Over | Just Getting Started | Can't Fight It

Standalone Titles:

Boy Trouble | Home to You

Acknowledgments

To Facebook Reader Group (Kaylee's Crew):

This book was for you. You voted on plot, main character names, careers, kids, and so much more. You guided this story. Thank you for taking this wild ride with me, and always supporting my books. I hope you love Laken and Grayson as much as I do.

To my family:

I love you. You hold me up and support me every day. I can't imagine my life without you as my support system. Thank you for believing in me, and being there to celebrate my success.

Lindee Robinson Photography:

I love this image! Thank you for being amazing at what you do and for another cover worthy image.

Tami Integrity Formatting:

Thank you for making the Perfect Embrace paperback beautiful. You're amazing and I cannot thank you enough for all that you do.

Sarah Paige—Opium House:

The covers for this series are stunning. You nailed our vision for this project.

My beta team:

Jamie, Stacy, Lauren, Erica, and Franci I would be lost without you. You read my words as much as I do, and I can't tell you what your input and all the time you give means to me. Countless messages and bouncing idea, you ladies keep me sane with the characters are being anything but. Thank you from the bottom of my heart for taking this wild ride with me.

Give Me Books:

With every release, your team works diligently to get my book in the hands of bloggers. I cannot tell you how thankful I am for your services.

Tempting Illustrations:

Thank you for your graphic skills.

Julie Deaton:

Thank you for giving this book a set of fresh final eyes.

Becky Johnson:

I could not do this without you. Thank you for pushing me, and making me work for it.

Marisa Corvisiero:

Thank you for all that you do. I know I'm not the easiest client. I'm blessed to have you on this journey with me.

Kimberly Ann:

Thank you for organizing and tracking the ARC team. I couldn't do it without you.

Stacy Garcia:

Thank you for your graphic talents. I would be lost without you!

Lacey Black:

You are my person. Thank you so much for being a constant confidant in this crazy book world. This might not be a co-written book, but you were still there every step of the way. I can't tell you how much I value our friendship.

Author Friends:

There are so many of you who are always there in my corner. Evan, Kelly, Catherine, Niki, Molly, and so many more. Thank you for being my tribe.

Bloggers:

Thank you, doesn't seem like enough. You don't get paid to do what you do. It's from the kindness of your heart and your love of reading that fuels you. Without you, without your pages, your voice, your reviews, spreading the word it would be so much harder if not impossible to get my words in reader's hands. I can't tell you how much your never-ending support means to me. Thank you for being you, thank you for all that you do.

With Love,